"That's better," he said in a lower tone. *"A real smile rather than a polite one."*

Their eyes locked. Time became suspended between one heartbeat and the next. For a moment, caught in those incredibly blue eyes that seemed to open clear to his soul, she relaxed her vigil. Warmth swept through her.

It was such an odd sensation that it took her a moment to recognize what it was and even longer to realize what had caused the acute stir of blood inside her.

An attraction. One that promised to be intense.

Her smile wavered. She wasn't here for either a fling or something more lasting. Her search for the truth of her past took precedence over everything else. Knowing that, she would leave and start a new life in a new place.

At least, those were her plans....

Dear Reader,

Welcome to more juicy reads from Silhouette Special Edition. I'd like to highlight Silhouette veteran and RITA® Award finalist Teresa Hill, who has written over ten Silhouette books under the pseudonym Sally Tyler Hayes. Her second story for us, *Heard It Through the Grapevine,* has all the ingredients for a fast-paced read—marriage of convenience, a pregnant preacher's daughter and a handsome hero to save the day. Teresa Hill writes, "I love this heroine because she takes a tremendous leap of faith. She hopes that her love will break down the hero's walls, and she never holds back." Don't miss this touching story!

USA TODAY bestselling and award-winning author Susan Mallery returns to her popular miniseries HOMETOWN HEARTBREAKERS with *One in a Million.* Here, a sassy single mom falls for a drop-dead-gorgeous FBI agent, but sets a few ground rules—a little romance, no strings attached. Of course, we know rules are meant to be broken! Victoria Pade delights us with *The Baby Surprise,* the last in her BABY TIMES THREE miniseries, in which a confirmed bachelor discovers he may be a father. With encouragement from a beautiful heroine, he feels ready to be a parent...and a husband.

The next book in Laurie Paige's SEVEN DEVILS miniseries, *The One and Only* features a desirable medical assistant with a secret past who snags the attention of a very charming doctor. Judith Lyons brings us *Alaskan Nights,* which involves two opposites who find each other irritating, yet totally irresistible! Can these two survive a little engine trouble in the wilderness? In *A Mother's Secret,* Pat Warren tells of a mother in search of her secret child and the discovery of the man of her dreams.

This month is all about love against the odds and finding that special someone when you least expect it. As you lounge in your favorite chair, lose yourself in one of these gems!

Sincerely,

Karen Taylor Richman
Senior Editor

Please address questions and book requests to:
Silhouette Reader Service
U.S.: 3010 Walden Ave., P.O. Box 1325, Buffalo, NY 14269
Canadian: P.O. Box 609, Fort Erie, Ont. L2A 5X3

The One and Only

LAURIE PAIGE

SPECIAL EDITION™

Published by Silhouette Books

America's Publisher of Contemporary Romance

For Russell, who, while not of the Dalton gang of Seven Devils Mountains, was a true hero when I needed one. Thanks for your help.
Laurie

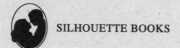 SILHOUETTE BOOKS

ISBN 0-373-24545-9

THE ONE AND ONLY

Copyright © 2003 by Olivia M. Hall

This edition published by arrangement with Harlequin Books S.A.

® and TM are trademarks of Harlequin Books S.A., used under license. Trademarks indicated with ® are registered in the United States Patent and Trademark Office, the Canadian Trade Marks Office and in other countries.

Visit Silhouette at www.eHarlequin.com

Printed in U.S.A.

LAURIE PAIGE

Along with her writing adventures, Laurie has been a NASA engineer, a past president of the Romance Writers of America, a mother and a grandmother. She was twice a Romance Writers of America RITA® Award finalist for Best Traditional Romance and has won awards from *Romantic Times* for Best Silhouette Special Edition and Best Silhouette. She has resettled in Northern California.

DALTON FAMILY TREE

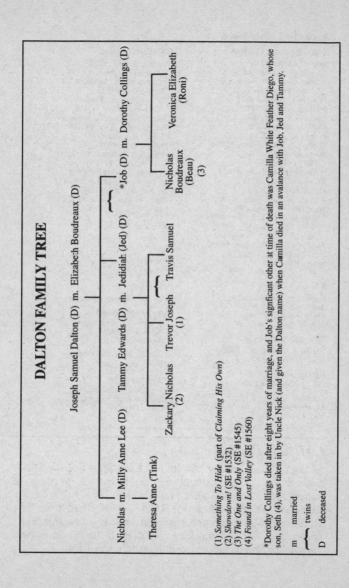

Joseph Samuel Dalton (D) m. Elizabeth Boudreaux (D)

Nicholas m. Milly Anne Lee (D)

Theresa Anne (Tink)

Tammy Edwards (D) m. Jedidiah (Jed) (D)

Zackary Nicholas (2)   Trevor Joseph (1)   Travis Samuel

*Job (D) m. Dorothy Collings (D)

Nicholas Boudreaux (Beau) (3)   Veronica Elizabeth (Roni)

(1) *Something To Hide* (part of *Claiming His Own*)
(2) *Showdown!* (SE #1532)
(3) *The One and Only* (SE #1545)
(4) *Found in Lost Valley* (SE #1560)

*Dorothy Collings died after eight years of marriage, and Job's significant other at time of death was Camilla White Feather Diego, whose son, Seth (4), was taken in by Uncle Nick (and given the Dalton name) when Camilla died in an avalanche with Job, Jed and Tammy.

m   married

⎨   twins

D   deceased

Chapter One

Shelby Wheeling smiled with the youngster as the doctor made a funny face at him, told him to say, "Ah," then checked his throat.

Dr. Dalton tossed the tongue depressor in the trash can. "For an old guy, you look pretty good to me. Don't forget to pick up a book on your way out," he said.

"To keep?" the boy asked.

"To keep," the doctor assured him.

The free checkup for all children entering kindergarten was a new program for the school, sponsored by the state, to see if it could nip problems in the bud and result in fewer absences for the new students.

"Tonsils," Dr. Dalton said to her after the child

left the room. ''Make a note to keep an eye out for strep infections and sore throats.''

Shelby quickly wrote the observations on the boy's chart and filed the chart in the special box provided by the state of Idaho for the Lost Valley School District. As the school nurse, it would be her duty to follow up on the doctor's orders.

New to the area, Shelby was still enthralled by the ''Wild West,'' as her parents back in the Low Country of South Carolina called the area. The Seven Devils Mountains arched spiny peaks into the blue bowl of the sky to the west of the valley. The Lost Valley reservoir eventually drained into the Salmon River, which ran into the Hells Canyon of the Snake River dividing Idaho from Oregon.

Rugged, mountainous land.

She glanced at the doctor as he helped a little girl up on the stool. Dr. Nicholas Boudreaux Dalton was handsome as sin, a beguiling devil with nearly black hair and eyes the color of the western sky. He'd asked her to call him by his nickname, Beau.

According to her landlady at the B and B, there were several other Daltons just as deadly gorgeous.

This particular one was very good with children, kind and teasing with the little ones, but all serious business with her. That suited her just fine.

She wasn't in town for romance. Far from it. She wanted to find her birth parents and to discover if any genetic disorders ran in the family. Her adoptive mom and dad worried about her getting hurt. They urged her to put the past behind her and to make a new life, but she needed to know this one thing for her own peace of mind.

"Say 'ah,'" the doctor told the girl.

"Ah," she mimicked, then she stuck her tongue out at him and crossed her eyes.

"Hold it," Dr. Dalton said, and pretended to take a picture. "We need to run a photo on the front page of the paper. 'Monster on the loose in Lost Valley. Can't see well, but may be dangerous. Tickling makes it disappear,'" he said as if quoting headlines.

The five-year-old giggled when he proceeded to give her a gentle tickle under her ear.

The childish laughter caused an instant flash of pain along Shelby's nerves, and with it, the regret and the terrible sense of loss.

Like now, the memories came at odd moments. She'd be fine, then some little thing—the delighted gurgle of a baby, the happy squeal of a child in a park, the closeness of a family having dinner in a restaurant—would throw her into the tangled web of the past.

The helplessness of watching her own child slip away from life returned like a hammer blow to her chest. Nine months of carrying the baby, a year of watching her slowly fade due to a metabolic disorder until she went into a coma for a day, then…then it was over, and Shelby was left with only the memories. And the regret.

"Okay, Kenisha, I think you'll be fine in school,"

Dr. Dalton said. ''Try not to give your teacher a heart attack with the monster face.''

The girl scrambled down from the stool and dashed into the reception room to pick out a book, her mother rushing to keep up with her.

''Her weight is low, off the bottom of the chart for her age and height,'' he said. ''I want her on a daily vitamin program. Put her down for recall in three months.''

Shelby heard the words, but they didn't register. She knew she should be writing something, but her hand didn't move across the page of the girl's chart.

''Shelby?''

She stared into the blue eyes, the handsome, serious face, but she didn't respond to the question. Locked someplace between the past and the present, it was as if she didn't exist in either time.

''Hold the fort,'' Beau said, sticking his head around the door frame and speaking to the volunteer who was directing the flow of children into the examining room of the clinic. ''Give us ten minutes to catch up.''

He closed the door, then poured two cups of coffee. ''Here. Drink this.''

He watched the new school nurse as he held the plastic cup out toward her. She blinked, looked from him to the cup, then accepted it. Her fingers trembled slightly.

''Did you eat breakfast?'' he asked.

She shook her head. A ghost of an apologetic smile

appeared and disappeared, flashing over her mouth so rapidly he wasn't sure he'd seen it. "I was running late. The alarm didn't go off. Fortunately, Amelia woke me."

Amelia was the owner of the local B and B. A thoughtful person, she'd sent some muffins to the clinic that morning for the staff. From Shelby's remarks, he assumed she was staying at the grand old Victorian.

"Low blood sugar," he diagnosed, although he was sure it was more than that. He made a point of not prying into other people's problems. Unless the person was a patient, of course, which she wasn't. "We'll take a break. Sit down for a few minutes."

"Yes, thank you," she said. She took a seat and sipped the steaming coffee.

Beau went into the staff room, snagged two muffins and two cartons of nonfat milk and returned. His assistant was sitting where he'd left her, her gaze on the peaks visible from the window.

She glanced his way. Her eyes were as blue as his own, but her hair was a flaming auburn, as straight and fine as silk thread. Caught with a blue band at the nape, it cascaded down her back like a flow of hot lava.

He'd wanted to touch it since meeting her last week for the preschool consultation with the state and county officials about the new program. Interest of a physical nature hummed through him. He mentally took a step back to observe his own reaction.

Yeah, he was interested. But he wouldn't act on it.

Inhaling deeply as he put the treat on the counter behind her, he caught the subtle scent of shampoo and soap and talc, but no added cologne or perfume.

Her face, with its hint of golden freckles, was free of makeup. Its shape was a classic oval, like those in pictures depicting saints and such. He wanted to run his fingers along her cheek to see if her skin was as soft and smooth as it looked. Normally flushed a healthy pink, she looked pale now. "Peaked," his uncle Nick would say.

"Eat," he said.

She did as told. He let the silence linger between them while they finished the snack. Slowly the color returned to her face. Serenity seemed to enclose her in a protective aura, a thing he'd noticed at their first meeting, as if she existed in a clear shell that the world couldn't penetrate.

Again, he felt the tug of interest, only this time it was centered on her character. Was she reserved by nature, or had life shaped her that way?

None of his business, he reminded the curious part of him. Theirs was a business relationship.

"Thank you. That was delicious." She wiped the corners of her mouth, smiled and stood. "Sorry, but what was I supposed to put on Kenisha's chart?"

"Her weight is rather low. That in itself isn't necessarily a problem, but I want to keep an eye on her. She's to get a daily vitamin. Let's see her again in three months."

"Right." She wrote the information and flagged the chart, all business again now that she'd eaten.

Beau decided his original diagnosis had been correct—she'd needed a break and something to eat. After tossing the plastic cup into the trash, he told the receptionist to continue sending the kids in.

Normally on a Wednesday he'd be helping Zack over at the resort they were building at the lake. Instead he'd spent the time in the office. He and several local citizens were donating their services through the clinic he'd opened in July, a month ago today, to the cause of children's health before they started school in a couple of weeks.

Restlessness assailed him. Another two hours and they would be finished for the day. Then he'd head for the lake.

Shelby, the new part-time school nurse, stored the file in the box and selected the next one. Her smile was all gentle welcome as the next child came through the door.

His heart kicked into gear with a hard, steady *th-thump* that added to the hum of sexual energy running through him.

Cool it, he advised his libido. He didn't mix business and pleasure, never had, never would. However he did have a proposition to put to her. He'd already decided to invite her out to lunch when they finished.

It was after twelve before the last of the youngsters in the new program were checked and pronounced fit.

The kids were also going through a battery of tests to determine their readiness for school. Welcome to the exciting world of learning!

"How about some lunch?" he said to Shelby.

She shook her head and closed the file box provided by the state. "I, uh—"

It was obvious she couldn't come up with a reasonable lie fast enough to account for a refusal. Her reluctance was a challenge. It wasn't often a Dalton was refused by a woman. However this wasn't the two-step of courtship.

"It's business," he assured her.

"Business?" she repeated, looking dubious.

Beau wondered if she was so used to mowing men down with a glance from those blue eyes and a toss of that flaming hair that she couldn't comprehend a straightforward business offer. "Yes. If you're available, I thought we could discuss it over lunch."

She looked so relieved, he was almost insulted. He concluded he must be losing his touch. True, it had been a coon's age since he'd dated. Opening the clinic here and turning over his office in Boise to another doctor had taken up a lot of time and energy. It was a move he'd been saving and planning for, for five years.

Thinking over the past week, he didn't think he'd given the new nurse any reason to distrust him. He hadn't made a single untoward move during the four meetings they'd had to set up the screening program for the schoolkids.

With rueful amusement, he wondered if that was the problem—she'd expected a pass and he hadn't delivered. The town gossips tended to paint the Daltons with the broad brush of conjecture and innuendo, recounting every escapade from their youth with delighted indignation to newcomers.

"I suppose that would be all right," she finally agreed after taking her own sweet time to think it over.

"Good. Let's go. I'm starving."

He escorted her to his old pickup. She glanced at the vehicle, then at him. He couldn't help but grin at her surprise. "The royal chariot," he intoned, opening the door for her with a grand sweep.

The August heat, trapped in the interior of the truck, rolled over them like a blast from a furnace.

"Whew, let's let it cool out a bit first," he suggested. He slid into the driver's seat and started the engine, then flipped the air conditioner on to maximum air.

She got in, fastened the seat belt and looked at him without a hint of expression on her Madonna-perfect face.

For the first time since first or second grade, he felt rattled by a female's stare. That she expected nothing and wanted nothing from him was obvious. Puzzling, too. He'd never had such a nonreaction from a member of the opposite sex. Well, so much for the famed Dalton charm.

Laughing silently at his somewhat dented ego, he

slammed the pickup door and headed for the lake. He wondered if she'd accept his proposition.

"How quaint," Shelby murmured, entering the restaurant with its rustic wooden interior when Beau held the screen door open for her.

"Sit anyplace you like," a young woman advised, smiling at them from the cash register. "I'll be with you in a jiffy."

"There's a place by the window," her handsome companion said, gesturing across the plank floor to the opposite side of the room. Since it was after the main lunch hour, there were only three other occupied tables at present.

Beau took her arm and guided her to a table commanding a view of the Lost Valley reservoir and the mountains beyond. When they were settled, the hostess brought menus over. "The special is barbecued beans on cornbread with salad or coleslaw. It's delicious," she told them. "Your waitress is Emma. She'll be with you shortly. May I bring you something to drink?"

"Iced tea, please," Shelby said.

While he echoed her order, she observed the scene beyond the large window. The sun emblazoned diamond dust over every leaf, every blade of grass, every ruffle of water in the lake, so that the whole world seemed to sparkle.

She sighed, filled with a sort of nostalgia now instead of the intense grief. Like the endless sweep of the waves at the seashore where she grew up, the mountains had a therapeutic effect on her soul, easing the pain of loss and the hopes that had once filled her eighteen-year-old heart.

If there was one thing she had learned since that youthful time, it was that life was relentless. She'd only to live one day at a time, then the next, and the next, and then somehow, a year went by, and another, and another.

The heart does go on.

Her companion dug some change out of his pocket. He lined up a penny, nickel, dime and quarter on the table between them. When she raised her eyebrows in question, he flicked a finger toward the coins.

"However much your thoughts are worth," he said. "Take your pick. Or all of them."

After the waitress delivered tall glasses of iced tea, Shelby looked over the change and selected the quarter. "It's the Kentucky commemorative quarter," she told him, holding it up so he could see. "My mother came from there. Her parents had a farm and boarded horses. She loves to ride and still does to this day. We always had horses when I was growing up."

"Do you like riding?"

She nodded, then added truthfully, "Not that I've done much for the past ten—no, eleven—years."

"We'll have to see if we can't change that. My family has a ranch near here with plenty of horses just lazing around and getting fat."

The low, sexy cadence of his words rippled with

easy affection as he mentioned the ranch. She knew he'd grown up there, raised by his uncle Nick along with five other Dalton orphans, his mother having died in childbirth and his father in an avalanche that also claimed his cousin's parents more than twenty-two years ago. Amelia at the B and B had told her this much.

The soft aura of regret enlarged to include him. He, too, had suffered loss. He, too, had gone on and made a life for himself.

Heavens, but she was sentimental today. She laid the quarter back in the line and turned her attention to a couple who strolled along the lake path.

Her companion pushed the quarter toward her and pocketed the rest of the change. "That was for sharing your thoughts. You've been pensive today. Do you miss your folks?"

She nodded, letting him think she might be homesick. Baring her soul to anyone wasn't her way.

"So why did you leave the civilized east and come out here to the wilderness?"

"I'm looking for a cowboy, of course. Isn't that the American icon of manly courage?" Her grin wasn't exactly sincere, but she managed to hang on to it.

"Ready?" the waitress, who looked as if she might be sweet sixteen, inquired.

Shelby ordered the special. The doctor did, too, but added barbecued beef on the side. When the girl was gone, he eyed her for a minute.

There was something about his serious manner that was appealing. He had depth to him. And a solid presence that a person could depend on.

A slight shudder rippled through her. Her husband, as youthful as she, had deserted her and their child after the first month of sleepless nights and worry. He'd been the boy next door and she'd had a crush on him for as long as she could remember. He'd promised he would always be there.

Always had been exactly ten months after the marriage.

Closing her eyes for a second, she willed the memories to fade back into the hazy mist of the past. What was done, was done. She opened her eyes to find Beau studying her with a somewhat quizzical expression.

He was probably wondering what made her tick, seeing that she tended to go off into a daze every little bit today. She'd better pay attention if she wanted to keep her job and do her research.

"Sorry," she murmured, "I was daydreaming. The mountains are so beautiful I find it hard not to simply stare at them. What did you want to talk to me about?"

"A job."

That surprised her. "Well, I already have one."

His smile was quick and somewhat wry. "It's part-time. I wondered if you might be interested in working at the clinic as my assistant in the mornings."

"I'm teaching health classes at the high school

three mornings a week. It's also part of the new program funded by the state.''

''Yeah, the weight problems of the average American family has hit the national conscience, it seems. Education is part of the solution. Exercise is the other side of the equation, in my opinion. Not that anyone has asked me.''

His laughter reminded her of soft mornings and quiet walks, of birdsong and the whispers of the wind through the pines, of the peace she'd experienced since arriving in this enchanted valley. She could almost forget she had a mission.

''A daily activity program will be part of my class,'' she told him, glad of an innocuous topic to discuss. ''Diets don't work for most people. Less than ten percent of those who diet keep the weight off a year later while those who stick to a regular exercise program do.''

''Right. Say, maybe we can incorporate some kind of program for our patients,'' he said.

She realized where her enthusiasm for healthy lifestyles was leading. ''I can't take on anything else at present. But thank you for thinking of me.''

He shrugged, irritation or disappointment flicking through the thoughtful blue eyes. Well, she couldn't live her life to please him. She had her own problems.

Her mom's worried gaze appeared in her mental vision, her eyes the same deep blue as hers so that most people thought they were truly mother and daughter by blood. Maybe she was wrong to come here, to want to find out what she could about her birth parents.

Putting the past behind her sounded simple, but if she ever married again, she had to know…before she could chance having other children.

The heart-hurting love and regret hit her again, as always when she thought of the precious life that she'd once held in her arms—

"You okay?"

She blinked and came back to the present. "Sorry. I keep going off the deep end today, don't I?" She laughed softly to indicate it was nothing serious, only spring fever or something like that.

Realizing she sounded nervous instead of amused, she took a sip of tea and fought for composure, building the wall around her emotions one stone at a time until she was safe behind it again. Their meal arrived, relieving her of the need for small talk until they were alone again.

"You're very good with the children," she told him. "Putting them on the stool while you sit on a chair puts them on the same eye level. That way you don't loom over them like some colossus."

His face lit up in pleasure. Her heart gave an odd hitch that disturbed her equanimity a bit.

"I hated getting shots when I was a kid," he said. "One doctor had my mom sit on a stool and hold me while he sat on another one to do the examination. He told me he had to give me a shot, but it wouldn't hurt as much as it had before. He was right. It didn't seem nearly so bad. Since then, I've tried to remember what it's like being a kid.''

She realized Beau would make a good father. A sigh forced its way past her lips. She hadn't picked well when it came to a father for her child. Her nineteen-year-old husband had panicked and run when he realized there were serious problems to be faced.

Her parents had taken her and their grandchild in. Because of them, she'd weathered the storm of anger and grief and regret. Due to their loving support, she'd come through the ordeal a stronger person. With their help, she'd gone on to nursing school so she, too, could assist others in times of need.

Glancing up, she met the fathomless gaze of her companion. A feeling that all would come right, that here in this rugged country she would find the answers she sought, spread over her like a golden light. She smiled.

His lips curved in response.

Her smile grew.

He chuckled. ''That's better,'' he said in a lower tone. ''A real smile rather than a polite one.''

Their eyes locked. Time became suspended between one heartbeat and the next. She hadn't trusted anyone outside her family since she was nineteen. Ten years. For a moment, caught in those incredibly blue eyes that seemed open clear to his soul, she relaxed her vigil. Warmth swept through her.

It was such an odd sensation that it took her a moment to recognize what it was and even longer to realize what had caused the acute stir of blood inside her.

An attraction. One that promised to be intense.

Her smile wavered. She wasn't here for either a fling or even something more lasting. Her search for the truth of her past took precedence over everything else. Knowing that, she would then leave and start a new life in a new place.

Those were her plans.

Chapter Two

Shelby was tired upon returning to the Lost Valley B and B that evening. After changing to a knit slacks outfit, she went to the large lobby and reception area. Several couples and a family with two children enjoyed the ambience of the common room.

The owner, Amelia Miller, called out a greeting upon seeing Shelby. "How did your day go with the kids?"

"Fine but tiring," Shelby admitted. She chose a glass of iced wine cooler and a plate of fruit, cheese and veggies, then sat at a table for two overlooking the back garden. "You must have a green thumb," she told her landlady when she stopped by the table.

"Nope, a dedicated gardener. I can do okay with African violets, but that's my limit."

"Join me if you have a moment," Shelby invited.

Amelia nodded. "Let me refill the fruit tray, then I will." She dashed off to the nether regions of the large Victorian that had been converted to a bed-and-breakfast.

Shelby watched the shadows lengthen over the lovely landscape. In the carriage house or barn or whatever it was behind the main house, she could see several people moving around. They appeared to be couples. Were they dancing?

Amelia returned with a glass of red wine. "Whew, I must be getting old or people are eating more. It's harder to keep up nowadays."

Since Amelia looked no more than a couple of years older than she was, Shelby ignored the age remark. She grimaced ruefully. "According to all reports, Americans are eating more."

"So how was your first day, really?" Amelia asked. "Did Beau Dalton give you a hard time? Did you get heart palpitations as all the local gals do around the Daltons?"

Her laughter was so merry that Shelby had to laugh, too. "He is good-looking, but he was also professional."

"Ah, yes. All the Daltons are dedicated to their jobs."

Shelby, not knowing the family, didn't comment. Instead she said, "He offered me a job in his office."

"Did he? I suppose he could use more help. He has a nurse practitioner who's also a midwife—she sees her own patients—and a receptionist who keeps the books, but he probably needs someone to assist him. It's difficult to get help in a small town.''

"Hmm," Shelby said noncommittally. "Has he been in business here long?"

"Before July he kept office hours in town, going from once to twice a week during the past year, but his main office was in the city. Last month he made the shift to here full time.''

Shelby had learned "the city" referred to Boise, which was over an hour's drive south of the valley. ''I see. Did he buy out another doctor's practice?''

"No. Doc Barony died about ten years ago.''

Shelby knew Beau was too young to have had a practice there very long, but she'd hoped he had taken over another's patients. That way, there might have been records going back several years, maybe to her birth.

''The house had been empty until Beau started up an office and brought in the midwife,'' Amelia continued.

''The house?'' Shelby asked, not sure what her landlady was talking about.

''Beau's office. It belonged to the old doctor. The attic is still full of records, the receptionist said. She's afraid the ceiling is going to fall in on her head.''

A jolt of excitement shot straight through Shelby. Records! Just what she wanted to get her hands on. But how?

Amelia finished her wine and stood. ''Well, back

to work. I see a new family arriving. How do you like your room? It's rather small, so I worry about claustrophobia.''

''I love it,'' Shelby assured the other woman, who had lovely auburn hair with golden highlights and a charming amount of natural curl, unlike her own flaming-red, string-straight locks that had been the scourge of her life.

With a satisfied nod, Amelia left. Shelby at once reverted to her own mission. If only she could accept Beau's offer of a job. No, she already had too much to do. Maybe she could volunteer to sort through the old records, keeping the ones for current patients.

Why would anyone in her right mind volunteer for such a job? She couldn't come up with a good reason.

A tall, masculine figure with dark hair and a smooth stride crossed a flagstone path, heading for the door near her table. Her heart gave an unexpected skip-thump-skip-thump before settling down when she realized the man was a stranger, one who looked awfully like Beau Dalton.

He paused as if hearing something, then turned, waiting for a lovely woman to catch up with him. She came from the carriage house, where, Shelby assumed, the man had also been. The door opened, admitting the couple and a wave of August air, hot and dusty to the senses.

Meeting the man's eyes, she saw they were as blue as the early evening sky. He had to be one of the infamous Daltons that Amelia had mentioned. He gave her a smile and nod. The blonde on his arm glanced her way.

"Are you the new school nurse?" she asked.

"Why, yes," Shelby said, unable to hide her surprise.

The young woman, about Shelby's age, held out a hand. "I'm Honey Dalton. This is Zack. Beau has mentioned working with you. Zack and Beau are cousins."

"I'm Shelby Wheeling." Shelby shook hands with both of them, giving Zack a wry smile. "You and your cousin look enough alike to be twins."

That brought a ripple of laughter from the couple. "We have those in the family, too," he explained. "My younger brothers are twins."

"Do they look like you and Dr. Dalton, too?"

"They do," Honey told her. "Get the four of them together and even I get confused."

"Yeah? Just don't let me catch you making out with one of the others," Zack threatened.

Noting their wedding rings and the easy air between them, Shelby concluded they were husband and wife. "Is something going on in the carriage house?" she asked, curious about the couples she saw leaving.

Honey nodded. "I'm holding dance classes there. That was the Wednesday afternoon couples class. Ballroom and modern dance. We would love to have you join us."

Shelby didn't know what to say.

"I need a partner," Zack assured her. "My wife

dances with all the other men on the pretext of showing them what to do and how to hold their partners.
I end up standing by the wall most of the time.''

''Uh, thanks, but I think I'd better get settled in a
bit more first. You wouldn't happen to know of any
apartments for rent, would you?''

Honey was sympathetic. ''It's hard to find a rental
in a small place like this. However, there's a cottage
by the lake next to the resort property,'' she said with
a tentative glance at her husband.

''It's for sale, not rent,'' he reminded her.

''I was wondering if they might rent it while waiting for a buyer. You know the owner. Think you
could ask him?''

Shelby perked up at this news. The only available
apartment in town had been over a gas station and
totally unacceptable in terms of cleanliness, repairs
and general livability. The extremely low rent had
been its only redeeming feature.

''No problem. I'll let you know,'' he told Shelby.

''Thanks. Would you leave word with Amelia if
I'm not in? I'll be teaching at the high school three
mornings each week when school starts, then doing
nurse duty at the elementary school in the afternoons.''

''Isn't this the loveliest place?'' Honey gestured
around the B and B common room. ''Amelia serves
the best breakfast rolls and pastries in town. Zack is
a deputy with the sheriff's department. Sometimes he
claims he has to stay over in town, but I know he

does it only so he can get a room here and have one of Amelia's breakfasts.''

He laid a hand over his heart. ''A man has to do his sworn duty.'' In an aside, he mock-whispered to Shelby, ''Honey always manages to stay over, too, and join me for breakfast and the evening snacks. She says it's my company she misses. A likely story.''

Laughing, they bid her goodbye and went to speak to the landlady before heading out the front door.

A funny pang, part nostalgia, part yearning, filled Shelby's chest so that it was difficult to breathe. Once she'd been like that couple—happy and confident and so very much in love, so sure of the future.

Now she could only shake her head at how naive she'd been at eighteen, fresh out of school and determined to marry her sweetheart. She hadn't been able to imagine anything bad happening to them.

Looking out at the golden grasslands beyond the lush garden, she realized she no longer imagined anything very wonderful happening in her future.

My, how pessimistic she had grown, she chided. Expect the worst so as not to be surprised when it happened. That was her motto. She had to smile.

''I'm sorry, Miss Wheeling, the funds didn't come through. We thought they had been promised, but someone misunderstood,'' the assistant superintendent of schools explained.

It was Monday morning and Shelby had reported in for the teachers' planning sessions at the high school, but had been referred to the superintendent's office instead.

"So there're no funds for a health teacher?" she repeated to make sure she understood. "What about the school nurse position in the afternoons?"

"We're okay on that," he assured her with a big smile. "Those funds come from a different pot."

"I see."

"I'm terribly sorry about all this," he continued. "We always need substitutes. Perhaps I could put you on the list?"

"Uh, let me think about it. I'll get back to you." She rose when he did, obviously dismissed.

Her ears ringing with his apologies, she left the building and drove from the county seat, where the high school and administrative offices were located, to Lost Valley. Considering her savings, she had enough money to make it here for a year without working at all, but work gave her a ready cover for her covert activities.

Arriving in town, she parked in front of the Victorian that housed the doctor's offices. She actually felt lighter as she walked up the steps and into the building. Now if the job with Beau was still open, all would be perfect.

He was at lunch, the receptionist told her. The office would be open at two. Disgruntled, Shelby retraced her steps and stood on the broad porch with its sweeping view of the three nearest peaks from which Seven Devils Mountains got its name.

He-Devil Mountain. She-Devil Mountain. The Devil's Tooth. Odd names that came from a Native American legend of seven monsters who had terrorized the land until Coyote turned them into mountains.

The monsters must have been made from copper for that was the most common ore in the area. Gold had been discovered near there in 1860.

She whimsically wished she could have lived then. To be a pioneer and brave the elements and the rugged wilderness, to find copper and gold, to found a homestead the way the Dalton ancestors had...

She sighed and shook her head at the romantic musing. Life had never been that idealistic.

"Get lost, cousin," Beau said.

Zack, startled, glanced toward the door of the restaurant. The Crow's Nest was a log-and-plank structure with a view of the reservoir that provided water for the small town of Lost Valley. The restaurant was deliberately rustic, but the scenery saved it from coyness. The food made it a draw for locals as well as visiting fishermen.

"Ah, the nurse," Zack said, spotting the lone female entering through the heavy plank door with its antler door handles. "Something going there, cuz?"

Beau grinned mysteriously. "I offered her a job last week. I think she may accept. The teaching job didn't get funded, so she might need extra income."

"Well, then, good luck. Time for me to return to

the harrowing life of a lawman, running down stray dogs, saving cats from trees and all that excitement.''

Zack rose, gestured for Shelby to join them and held out a chair. "Hey, pretty lady," he called. "You're just in time. I'm Zack. We met at Amelia's last week.''

"I remember. You and Honey," she said.

When she was seated, he winked over her head at Beau, then ambled out to the sheriff's department cruiser assigned to him as a deputy.

"Oh, did I interrupt?" she asked.

"Not at all," Beau said, enjoying the flash of fire in her hair as she watched his cousin depart. She turned back to him.

Man, but she was beautiful. He couldn't remember the last time he'd seen a woman with so much natural beauty. Heavenly eyes. Gorgeous hair. Skin like the peaches and cream of song and poem.

His fingers actually tingled with the urge to reach out and touch…and get his face slapped in the process. That clear shell, like an enchanted glass bubble, surrounded her as fully as a suit of armor.

"Have you had lunch?" he asked.

She shook her head.

He signaled for a menu to the teenager who was waiting tables today. "Grilled chicken was the special. I can recommend it.''

For some reason it pleased him that she followed his suggestion. "The raspberry iced tea," she finished.

"So, how was your morning?" he asked.

She visibly hesitated, then said, "Well, that depends on how you look at it."

Her smile was unexpected, a gift that sent warmth scurrying around inside him. Another surprise. He didn't know why she had such an effect on him. But there it was.

"Tell me how you look at it," he invited.

When she explained about the teaching job, he nodded. "You knew?" she asked.

"I saw the high school principal over the weekend. He was angry at the budget cut and the loss of the classes. He thought the school administration had been unfair to you. Is that the way you feel?"

Impish dimples appeared at the corners of her mouth. "Not if the position in your office is still open."

His gaze fastened on the dimples. He thought of kissing her there, then continuing on to the soft, pink mouth. A buzz of sexual interest hummed through his blood.

Her smile faltered.

He forced himself to lighten up. "Uh, yes, the position is still open. Does this mean you'll take it?"

The dimples returned. "Tell me the hours and the pay first."

"Hmm, going to drive a hard bargain, are you?" He raised one eyebrow in mock challenge. "You won't get a better offer in town. Most women would snap it up."

She laughed out loud. "How much?" she demanded. "How long?"

"From eight until noon on days you have to report to the elementary school. Eight to five on days you don't. We're closed on Wednesdays, open a half day on Saturday if it's busy, which it probably won't be in winter."

She shook her head. "I'll be at school every afternoon."

"But only until three. You could come over for a couple of hours after that."

"Let me get settled into the school routine first, then I'll think about the afternoons. Only mornings now."

He went through the same two-step with her over salary. She opted for hourly pay with time-and-a-half if she worked on Saturdays. He agreed, thinking he got a bargain. It was impossible to find professional help in the area. He'd lucked out.

"So how did you happen to come to town?" he asked after her lunch was served and his cup refilled with fresh coffee.

"I wanted to live someplace different. When I saw a notice for a school nurse here and looked the town up on the map, I thought this was the place."

"Where did you see the notice?"

"On the Internet."

"I see. Then?"

"Then I responded to the ad, found out it involved teaching and, since I had teaching credentials for first

aid, health and beginning nursing care, I was accepted.''

"Some of the cowboys who came to town Friday
night were real glad when they saw you walking on
the path by the lake. We don't get many redheaded
beauty queens here.''

Again she laughed, and again the heat flowed like
sweet, warm honey through him.

"I think I'm glad, too,'' he murmured.

Her eyes met his, widened, then looked away. "I
don't date the boss,'' she said with prim modesty.

"Neither do I. But dinner with a colleague is
okay.'' Glancing at the wall clock—a picture of the
mountains painted on a polished pine slab with the
dial mounted at the corner—he found it was time to
be getting back. "Duty calls,'' he said. "Can you
start in the morning?''

"Yes. I'll be there. At eight.''

"Good.'' He paid the bill for both of them over
her protests. "Consider it a welcome luncheon,'' he
told her, feeling jaunty and pleased about their deal,
before heading to the office for afternoon hours.

There was something intriguing about the new
school nurse, something he couldn't quite put a finger
on. A mystery. Perhaps she'd come here because she
was running from something. A painful past? A pos-
sessive boyfriend? A scandal? There were lots of pos-
sibilities.

Washing up before seeing his afternoon patients,

he considered the careful distance she maintained from others. He'd always been a sucker for a challenge.

Returning to the B and B upon finishing her lunch, Shelby stepped over the threshold and paused. There seemed to be a meeting going on.

"Come on in," Amelia called. "We're having a committee meeting, part of the Historical Society."

"We can use all the help we can get," one very elderly lady told her, the lines in her face all crinkling at once into a charming, ageless smile.

"Grab a glass of tea and some cookies," Amelia advised. "This is going to be a long session."

Shelby was pulled into the group of four women and found herself seated, sipping tea and earnestly considering the committee's project—compile a brief historical listing of all the old families who had settled the area, where they'd come from, who their descendants were, and how many generations were represented.

"A sort of genealogy of the valley," Amelia concluded two hours later. "I think it will have to be tied to the land as land titles are usually the most common records."

"Exactly," the elderly lady said, beaming.

Shelby learned Miss Pickford, president of the Historical Society, was also descended from a First Family of Idaho, as were the Daltons. The woman was almost eighty, had taught in a two-room school in the county, had retired fifteen years ago, was kin to the Daltons and nearly everyone else in the area, and was universally loved. She had blue eyes and lovely silver hair and a soft, thoughtful way of speaking that made one instinctively trust her.

After the meeting broke up, Shelby and Amelia lingered over fresh glasses of tea and chatted about the task ahead.

Amelia laughed softly. "Welcome to the newest member of the Historical Society." She toasted Shelby with her glass.

"I don't know how that happened," Shelby admitted with more than a hint of wry humor.

"I do," her landlady said confidently. "Miss Pickford could get money and a pledge to participate in a Christmas toy fund-raiser from the Grinch."

"I think you're right. We need to find out about her early teaching days here," Shelby said thoughtfully. "She must know tons of interesting stories and anecdotes."

"Hmm, she could probably blackmail ninety percent of the population over the age of thirty since she taught most of them. My parents had her when the school board opened the elementary school here for one through eighth grades and closed all the county schools."

A bolt of excitement shot through Shelby. The teacher might have known *her* parents, too. Her mother could have been a student who got pregnant and went away to have the baby, perhaps living with relatives in South Carolina and giving the baby up for adoption there.

She took a calming breath, aware that she was letting her imagination run wild. One thing at a time.

Amelia snapped her fingers. "Old Doc Barony's records!"

"In the attic," Shelby added, following the line of thought perfectly.

"Yes. In your spare time…" Amelia said, giving her a big grin, "maybe you could record the names of patients—oh, and the dates any of them died and any children born—then we could compare those to the county title records to make sure we got everyone."

Shelby's heart went into a series of rapid beats. Birth. Death. Names. Dates. Diseases and disorders. Those records might tell her everything she needed to know.

"That's a possibility," she said, careful to keep her voice blandly interested.

"You'd have to ask Beau, but I don't see any reason he'd refuse. I mean, you're a nurse, so you'd keep everything confidential."

"Right," Shelby said. "In fact, I'm going to be working for Dr. Dalton. In the mornings." She explained all that had happened that day—the canceling of the health classes and her acceptance of Beau's offer.

"Perfect," Amelia declared, rising. She glanced at her watch. "Time to start preparing the evening snacks. I have a new recipe for crab-apple dip, as in seafood mixed with fresh chopped apples, that I want to try tonight. Come to the kitchen and we can talk while I cook.''

Shelby followed her new friend into the spacious kitchen. The cook who did the breakfast menu was gone for the day, and the two younger women had it to themselves.

''Here, taste this and see if it has too much chili powder.'' Amelia handed her a cracker with a generous dollop of the dip.

''I think it's delicious. Shall I start on a vegetable tray or something?''

''Sure. In that big refrigerator, bottom drawer.''

After a few minutes of peeling and arranging, Shelby murmured, ''This is nice. It makes me sort of miss my mom, though. She and I always cooked together.''

''My mother and I were a disaster together,'' Amelia admitted. ''She never thought I did anything right.''

''That's too bad,'' Shelby said sympathetically.

Amelia sighed. ''She was right about some things. I married a handsome rodeo cowboy I'd known for all of two weeks, suffered two miserable years of marriage, then left him when he actually hit me once. In the meantime, my grandparents died within a few years of each other and I inherited this place. I was glad to tuck my tail between my legs and come here to live.''

"You've created a wonderful B and B," Shelby said sincerely. "You make all your guests feel welcome."

"It's because I'm happy. I learned home is truly where the heart is, and this is mine."

For a minute Shelby wanted desperately to bare her soul to Amelia and to tell her of her own past mistakes and her present quest. She hesitated, the phone rang and the moment was lost.

That was probably better anyway. She didn't want the information about her search leaking. If her birth mother still lived here, she didn't want to expose her to the embarrassment of her neighbors knowing about the child she'd given up twenty-nine years ago.

After having her own child and losing it, albeit to death, she didn't want to cause pain to anyone else. Setting the finished tray in the fridge, Shelby waved to the other woman and went to her room.

She considered the old records in the attic at Beau's office. They might tell her everything she needed to know without her having to search for a living person.

Tomorrow she would start work for Beau Dalton. She would ask him about going through the records for the Historical Society and volunteer to dispose of them. She considered this plan from all angles and decided it had no problems that she could see.

A picture of intense blue eyes flashed into her mind, eyes that seemed to see right inside her at times. She would have to compose her request beforehand so that she didn't stumble over the words and arouse his suspicions.

She wondered if he believed her story of finding out about the position here over the Internet.

It was true…as far as it went.

But, of course, it wasn't the whole story. She'd known exactly where she was going to look for a job.

The town was the only thing she knew about her birth mother. A copper bracelet had been forgotten and left at the birthing clinic. It had been made by a Nez Perce family and sold through a gift shop here in Lost Valley. The nurse had put it with her belongings when her adoptive parents had come to pick her up.

Shelby removed the bracelet from her small jewelry carrier, a velvet roll-up bag with several pockets her aunt, one of her father's sisters, had given her at graduation years ago. The copper gleamed brightly in the afternoon light from the window. Its polished stones were engraved with intricate symbols, similar to Egyptian scarabs but using birds and plants for models.

She didn't think her parents had been Native American, but that was a possibility. After considering wearing the bracelet, she reluctantly put it away. She had no idea whether anyone might recognize it, but she wasn't ready to take that chance. Not yet.

With a rueful smile, she admitted she'd learned caution in her old age. Her birth mother must have learned it, too.

The lines from a poem studied long ago came to her.

I was young, as was my heart;
And I followed where it led—
Followed my heart and not my head,
Those days
When I was young, as was my heart.

Some wistful part of her longed to be that young, confident girl again, excited about life and all that it could hold.

A more cynical part of her scoffed at the idea.

She knew which part to believe.

Chapter Three

Shelby didn't like the way her insides got all in a knot when she parked at the far end of the paved area beside the Lost Valley Medical Clinic. The first day on a new job was always nerve-racking, but she'd worked with many doctors in many situations at the hospital in her hometown. Today was no different from any other.

Except that she would be working with Beau Dalton and her reasons weren't purely medical.

Well, she couldn't sit in the car all day. Still, she hesitated for another few seconds. Scolding herself for being a coward, she climbed out of her subcompact station wagon and went inside.

"Hi," Beau greeted from the door to his office. "I

was wondering if you were going to come inside or if you'd changed your mind already.''

The receptionist wasn't in sight, so Shelby assumed they were alone. Perhaps this was an opportunity to mention the old files. She took a calming breath, then started. ''I haven't changed my mind. In fact, I've been sent on a mission here.''

He gestured toward his office. ''We have a few minutes. Come in and tell me about it.''

She glanced over his bookcases and briefly studied the diplomas and plaques that doctors acquired during their years of training. He'd taken courses in both diagnostics and surgery procedures, making him well qualified for a general practice in a small town.

''Do you approve?'' he asked in some amusement.

''Very much. Are you planning on doing surgery here?''

''Only for emergencies. I have arrangements with a surgeon in Boise to perform scheduled operations. You were going to tell me about your mission?''

''Oh, yes.'' She explained about the Historical Society and its needs.

''The old records,'' he murmured, his eyes on her. ''The attic is full of 'em. You know, that's a good idea. I'll help you go through them so we don't miss any of the founding fathers and mothers, then we'll shred the files.''

She was sure he didn't realize he was staring at her while he considered, but she was very aware of that deep blue gaze burning holes in her skin. Electricity zinged along every nerve, so much so that she hardly registered his decision to help her. Then it hit her.

"Oh," she said. "Uh, you don't have to help. I mean, all that dust to be stirred up. And it'll probably take a lot of time."

He merely nodded. "It'll be interesting, checking the old records. I'm familiar with most of the original families, so that should speed things along."

She realized to protest further would arouse suspicion. He was too quick on the uptake to deceive. Not that she was doing anything wrong. At least she didn't think she was. So why did she feel sneaky and underhanded?

Answer—the clear blue gaze that stared right into her soul. She looked away with an effort.

He reached over and stroked gently along her cheek. She whipped around, startled.

"I just had to see if your skin was as soft as it looked. It is," he told her.

His smile wasn't bold or teasing or sardonic. Instead he seemed pensive and lost in his own thoughts as questions flickered through his eyes. Some part of her also questioned the awareness between them and what it meant.

"I think," he said in a husky tone, "that together we may be flint and steel."

He touched the hair at her temple, then, without losing contact, moved his hand until he curled a finger under her chin and lifted her face so he could study her more closely.

Alarm whipped through her. "No," she whispered.

He raised his eyebrows slightly, as if amused by the odd play between them. "No?"

Their eyes met and held. A door opened and footsteps sounded in the hall. The moment shattered like dropped crystal. "Hello?" a feminine voice called.

"In here," he called. "It's Ruth Stein. Have you met her?" he asked Shelby.

During the next few minutes Shelby met Ruth, the nurse-midwife, a woman in her late forties who was married to one of the two brothers who owned the hardware store. The receptionist was Alberta Stein, married to the other brother and also in her mid to late forties.

That's where the similarity ended, Shelby noted. Ruth was close to six feet tall and pleasingly plump. Bertie, as the other was called, topped the chart at maybe five-two and a hundred pounds. Shelby, in the middle at five-five and average weight, was amused to see they formed a perfect set of stair steps as they shook hands and exchanged greetings.

"Why do I suddenly feel outnumbered?" Beau demanded, managing to appear worried about his safety.

"Because you are," Ruth assured him. "You'd better behave yourself in this office."

"I promise to curb my wilder tendencies." He cut a glance at Shelby. "Although I make no such claims for when we're outside office hours."

A sizzle of undefined emotion rushed along her nerves as the two older women followed his gaze, then smiled at her with speculation as well as kindness in their eyes.

"She's pretty, isn't she?" Beau said conversationally.

"Very much so," Bertie agreed.

"Watch him," Ruth advised. "If he gives you any trouble, let us know."

"I will," Shelby promised as the other three laughed with the easy camaraderie of those long known to each other. "You know, I think I'm going to like it here." She couldn't resist giving her boss a challenging sideways glance.

"You women," he scoffed, then ducked into his office as the phone rang. "I'll get it."

"Time to start work," Bertie said cheerfully, going to her desk at the front of the office.

Shelby realized it was exactly eight o'clock. The day had truly begun. She wondered when she could get at the files in the attic.

At five that afternoon Shelby hung up the phone on her last call. She'd completed all the follow-up calls to the parents of those students who needed additional care per Beau's instructions, so all was in order for school to start in two weeks. Since she didn't have classes, she technically had no other duties until that time.

Returning to the B and B, she changed to shorts, tank top and jogging shoes, then headed for the path on the other side of town. There, she noticed all the new building going on around the lake formed by the reservoir dam as she jogged along the trail.

Most of the houses were impressive, and she wondered how so many people had the money to build such large homes. She gazed wistfully at the cottage that was for sale next to a large building that looked as if it would be a resort. Her heart dipped when she saw a Sold sign on the tiny house.

"Hey, hello!"

She stopped in surprise when Beau Dalton yelled and waved her over. Going to where he and a couple of other men worked on the foundation of the resort, she couldn't help but gasp when the trio smiled at her.

She couldn't recall ever being in the presence of three more dynamic men, all of them similar in their blue-eyed, dark-haired good looks, two of them as alike as the proverbial peas. They all wore old cargo shorts or cutoffs with sneakers and no shirts.

Bronzed, broad-shouldered and slim-hipped, they exuded masculine power and confidence. She found herself wary, on guard against the overwhelming aura of force they unconsciously represented.

Beau gestured to the other two. "My cousins, Travis and Trevor. And yes, they're twins."

"Glad to meet you," one of the twins said.

"Ditto," the other said with decidedly more enthusiasm, unbridled interest leaping into his eyes.

Shelby felt a bit flustered.

"Down, boy," Beau said to his cousin. "Trev is a nuisance, but harmless," he then assured her.

"Pay no attention," Trevor advised. "He's just jealous of my charm and wit."

"Ha," Beau scoffed. "I once heard a teacher tell him that each time he opened his mouth, general knowledge decreased proportionally."

Smiling and nodding, she listened to their easy teasing and wished she'd had cousins like these. Trevor took her arm and urged her toward the structure they worked on.

"Lies, all lies," he said. "Would you like a tour of the lodge?"

"Well, uh, yes. I think," she amended with exaggerated uncertainty.

Beau swept her away from his cousin. "I need to discuss business with her," he said loftily.

Trevor sighed in disgust, grinned at her, then returned to work with his twin, setting a foundation sill in place.

Beau, still holding her wrist, led her toward the cottage. "Zack said you were interested in the cottage."

"I was hoping I could rent it. But it's sold."

Dropping her arm, he stepped onto the small brick porch with its charming white columns and rails and unlocked the door. "Enter," he invited with a grand sweep of his hand.

She did so. "Oh," she murmured in delight. "It's as lovely as I thought it would be."

A half wall divided the living room from the kitchen. White wainscoting in beadboard lined the bottom third of the rooms. Stenciled vines on pale golden walls framed windows and doors. White curtains, looking as freshly washed and starched as her grandmother's, wafted in the breeze from the mountains. The furniture was mismatched, well-used and simply wonderful.

"You like?" he asked.

"Yes. It reminds me of home. My mother and I stayed with my grandmother a couple of weeks each summer. Her house was like this."

Her throat closed and she had to stop. Her grandmother had died last summer and the house had been sold.

"You miss them," he said, his voice deep, rich with understanding that added to her sudden emotion.

She managed a smile. "Yes."

"Going off on an adventure seems exciting, but then you realize how far you are from home. I went to medical school back east. It was hell."

Nodding, she continued the tour, needing to escape his kindness and the yearning that bloomed in her like a weed in an orderly garden. She wasn't here for this.

The kitchen was pale green with white woodwork and yellow accents in a wall clock and the cushions on ladder-back chairs. It was the windows she liked best. Covering most of the back wall, they showed off the view to perfection—lake and mountains and blue, blue sky. A bit of heaven tucked into this high valley.

The bedroom was the only other room. It and a rather large bathroom occupied the other side of the house. The bed, rocking chair, table and armoire were oak. A dustcover protected the queen-size bed that was so high it needed two oak steps to get to it.

The ceiling was vaulted and covered with white-washed beadboard. A fan was mounted high in the center of it. The walls were creamy beige, again with attractive stencils, but of climbing roses in yellow and pink shades this time.

"Lovely," she murmured. Her voice was a husky whisper, sounding loud in the silent house. She swallowed, suddenly nervous about being here with this alluring man.

"Yes."

His voice was unexpectedly close. She glanced over her shoulder and found him only inches away. Slowly she turned.

Her eyes were on a level with his chest. The curly hair there was coal-black, scattered sparsely over his bronzed skin. The defined pectoral muscles flexed once, then went still as she stared at this monument to human male perfection. She lifted a hand, then stopped.

He caught her hand and pressed it flat against him.

The air became heavy, expectant. She had to open her mouth to get it into her lungs. She raised her eyes from the well-developed pecs to his throat, then upward, until she gazed at his mouth. Longing, sharp and poignant, filled her.

"Do it," he said in a low, strained tone.

"What?" She hardly knew what she said.

"What your eyes are saying you want."

"I don't...want..." She didn't continue because she didn't know what she wanted...no, because she knew what she *shouldn't* want, but did.

"I do," he murmured. "I want to touch you."

His lips touched hers, soft, dry, a fleeting brush of mouth over mouth. She licked her lips. His eyes, when she looked up, were dark and mysterious deep blue pools to drown in. She yearned to dive in, to never leave.

No. It was a mistake to give in to desire and let passion lead her into temptation. Once she'd mistaken a romantic dream for a lasting love. She wasn't so foolish now. She reminded herself of all she'd learned from the past. Hearts were fragile things. They could break again, and again, and yet again.

He moved his hand, slowly caressing her face with fingers that trembled ever so slightly. The passion dazzled, beckoned from his dark, heated gaze.

Fear stirred through her, warning her of the danger. "Dr. Dalton," she said, the beginning of a protest.

"Beau," he corrected, and removed the band from her hair. He pushed it into his pocket, then spiked his fingers into the freed tresses, cupping his broad, gentle hands around her skull and holding her still when she would have turned away from those eyes, that mouth.

"Beau," she said, and wondered why she did and how it could feel so right on her tongue. "Beau."

So old-fashioned, Beau, with an innocent ring of days long ago. When she'd been young, she would have believed in that innocence.

"Yes," he said. "Yes."

The kiss wasn't a simple brushing of lips over lips this time. It was man to woman, all heat and demand and whimsical yearning.

The impact went all the way down to her toes, something she couldn't recall ever experiencing before, not with this intensity, these flashes of fire that burned and ached within until she wanted to cry out.

With a gasp she opened to him, letting the kiss go deeper, until she was filled with it. Wonder washed through her and took all traces of fear with it. Breathing became difficult, then unnecessary.

When he at last released her mouth, he laid a trail of flame along her cheek. "You have the smoothest skin. I've wanted to touch you since that first meeting, to see if the fire in your hair was in your blood."

"Is it?"

"Yes. Heaven help me, yes," he said.

But she knew who needed help here. Sanity returned through the foggy haze of hunger. She laid her hands flat against his chest, then lingered to caress the hair-roughened skin. "We shouldn't do this."

"Why not?"

She forced herself to search for a reason even as she continued to touch him. "You're my boss."

"We're colleagues."

"We work in the same—"

"Shh," he ordered, but softly, his voice a caress, too.

"I know this isn't wise." She wished she didn't sound so desperate.

"I agree."

Running his hand under her tank top, he rubbed across her back, trailing his fingers into the indentation of her spine and sliding them up and down. He explored farther.

"Where's the catch?" he asked.

"It's a sports bra. There isn't one."

"Oh."

He explored the cotton material with his sure, skillful touch that sent cascades of sensation down, down, down into her. Excitement grew as she experienced the enticing movement of his hard body against hers.

The rainbow hues of mutual need slowly overtook her as they kissed again, then again, each time more deeply, more intimately. He skimmed her breasts, then cupped them in his palms and rubbed his thumbs along the hard points that formed under his touch.

The sounds of a hammer next door disappeared. The lazy drone of a fly against the window became but an odd counter-beat to the drumming in her heart.

"Never thought I'd feel this," he said, pushing her top up and staring at the outline of her nipples against the gray cotton of her sports bra. He looked into her eyes. "I never knew hunger could be this strong."

She couldn't look away from the blazing need. "It's too strong," she protested softly. "Too much, too soon."

"But it's there."

His gaze dared her to deny it. She couldn't. "I don't want to feel this."

"Then stop it," he said, mocking her. He nibbled at her breasts through the cloth. "I can't." He pressed his face into the valley between her breasts and inhaled deeply. "But then, I don't want to."

Before she quite realized what was happening, he took a step, then another. She stepped back with him, following as if they engaged in some strange dance, accompanied by the mad music in her blood, that took them wherever it would.

When she felt the bed behind her knees, she realized, with a stricken jolt, exactly where they were going.

"Beau..." she said raggedly, pushing against him.

Her voice sounded reedy and uncertain. She shook her head when he bent to her mouth once more. He clasped her hands, moved them behind her, pulling her close, and took her mouth in a kiss that demanded total participation.

Panic eddied through her blood even as electricity arced between them. This had to stop. She had to...to breathe, but she couldn't...she couldn't think...

Her thoughts were like a flock of wild birds, whirling and swirling through her mind too swiftly and too frightened to come to the perch of reason. She struggled to free her hand, got one loose and, twisting, raked down his chest with her fingernails—an instinctive act of self-preservation.

His head jerked up. They stared at one another.

Slowly he released her and backed up a step. The breath rushed into her lungs, making her dizzy.

Glancing down, he observed the four red lines standing in ridges on his skin. He turned his gaze from them to her. "No woman has ever marked me before," he said, not in anger or accusation, but as if in deep thought, as if wondering about the marks— how they'd happened and why.

Pressing her shaky hands against her breast, she confessed, "I've never done anything like that. I don't know why I did. It…it was like I couldn't breathe. Everything was going dark." She stopped because she didn't know how to explain the unexplainable.

He smiled and it was full of gentle irony. The ache inside her returned. "I don't think I've ever frightened a woman before, certainly not like this." He touched her cheek with exquisite tenderness. "It's strong, isn't it?"

She clasped her arms over her middle and nodded.

"This hunger," he continued as if thinking out loud. "It's different, more than I've ever experienced, so much so that I didn't get your signals at first."

"Signals?"

"The panic," he reminded her softly, and rubbed across her lips with one finger, then dropped his hand and stepped back another foot, giving her room. "I was too lost..." He hesitated, then shook his head. "That's never happened to me before—to get so lost in passion that everything else disappeared. It'll be different next time," he promised.

She moved sideways until she was on a line for the door. She hurried toward it. She managed to laugh and pretend it was all a joke. "I don't think we should attempt a next time."

"I do."

The words were barely audible as she rushed across the charming living room and out the front door. The hammering at the resort stopped. She stared distractedly at the twin brothers, who stared back with frank interest.

The door closed behind her.

"Do you want the place?" Beau asked. "I'll keep the rent reasonable."

"You?" she questioned, turning from the stares next door.

"I bought the cottage. It seemed a good idea since it was next to the lodge. The new homeowners might have given us trouble over parking or noisy guests."

She tried to think clearly. "Perhaps it would be best if—" She faltered on the brink of refusing the offer. She glanced at the cottage and knew she still wanted it.

"Good. Do you need help moving in?"

"No."

"Okay. I have to get back to work. See you in the morning. I'll give you a key then."

She blinked and realized he thought she had accepted. But why shouldn't she rent it? It was charming. It fit her needs. She would have it to herself. She followed him down the flagstone path to the road. "Wait, the rent," she reminded him. "How much?"

"Two hundred a month."

She stopped. "That's a steal."

He grinned over his shoulder. "So maybe you'll feel guilty enough to invite me over for a home-cooked meal once in a while."

With that, he strode across the grass and got back to work. His cousins looked at her, then him. Feeling that they knew every intimate touch that had occurred between her and Beau, she swung toward town and jogged back to the B and B as calmly as possible.

"Will you look at that?" Trevor said in awe.

Beau gave him a warning glare. He looked around, spotted his T-shirt and put it on.

"What happened while you were showing a prospective renter the house?" Trev demanded.

"Nothing," Beau muttered, tightening a bolt against the mud sill.

Trevor looked at his watch. "Less than fifteen minutes," he remarked. "Man, I wish I could make a woman so mad with passion in that length of time that she was clawing my body."

"Yeah," Beau agreed. "You should be so lucky."

Travis, the quiet twin, grinned.

"Not going to tell us about it, huh?" Trevor, the irrepressible cousin, demanded.

"Not a bit."

"Well, at least you got a trophy during the battle."

Beau glanced down and spotted the blue headband dangling from his pocket. He shoved it out of sight.

Trevor continued his lament. "I was hoping for a few pointers. My love life sure isn't anything to write home about. Have you noticed how few women our age live around here? You two have grabbed the prettiest ones to show up in a coon's age."

Beau glanced at Travis. The twin had recently gotten engaged to Alison, who'd come to town looking for her long-lost sister, who was pregnant and living with the owner of the ranch next to the Dalton homestead sans marriage.

Uncle Nick, who had raised the Dalton orphans, approved of the engagement and disapproved of loose living and having children out of wedlock.

Beau considered what had nearly happened in the cottage. He'd never had an experience exactly like that.

Life took on some added complications as he tried to figure out what had happened between him and Shelby. The nail marks on his chest tingled as if trying to tell him. They hadn't been deep enough to break the skin, but they had made an impression on him.

No woman had ever had to fight her way out of his arms in the past. He wondered what that brief loss of control said about him and the gentleness Uncle Nick said men had to maintain around women.

He shook his head, as he marvelled at the strength of the attraction between them, knowing it wasn't all on his side. He wasn't sure what it meant…not sure at all.

Chapter Four

Saturday afternoon Shelby glanced around the small bedroom, then, just to be sure she hadn't forgotten anything, she rechecked every drawer and looked under the bed, easy chair and desk. Nothing there.

She carried her last bag to the car, stowed it in the back and slammed the rear lid.

"I'm going to miss you," Amelia said, coming out of the B and B and crossing the lawn to the gravel parking area.

Shelby nodded and returned her landlady's smile. "When I'm settled, I'll have you over for tea. If I can wheedle some recipes out of your cook. She makes the best pastries I've ever eaten."

"Isn't she wonderful? I've tried to get her to open

her own coffee shop, but she says no. Who am I to argue myself out of the best cook I've ever known?''

"Good thinking," Shelby agreed. "Okay, I'm off. I feel rather like Dorothy, off to find the Wizard of Oz."

Amelia watched her go and with a final wave, went back inside. Shelby drove down the pleasant side street, turned north on Main and drove across town to the cottage by the lake. It took all of five minutes.

Her heart thumped noisily when she parked under the shelter of the carport attached to the tiny house. As she retrieved her luggage, she noticed the work going on next door. Since last Tuesday, the framework of the walls had gone up.

Several men, mostly young and dressed in shorts and sneakers or work boots, swarmed over the site. Pausing as she unloaded her car and carried her belongings inside, she watched as a concrete truck backed into place. The Dalton twins and two other men spread the wet mix over what appeared to be a huge patio at the back of the building.

One of the twins waved, sending her a big smile.

Trevor, she thought. Travis was the other. Zack was their brother, Honey was his wife. There were two other Daltons, one of which was Beau's sister. The patriarch was their uncle Nick, a man of wisdom and kindness that Beau spoke of with great affection.

Shelby realized she was coming to know the Dalton gang. Not positive this was a good thing, she continued with her work. An hour later her things were stored, the bed was made and the refrigerator was humming.

The next thing on her list was food. The town had one supermarket and one organic grocery that advertised ''natural'' foods. She bought her staples at the market and some local-grown fruit at the other. Returning to the cottage, she spotted a masculine figure that, to her, stood out from all the other handsome examples of healthy, powerful males next door.

Beau came over and hefted two bags of groceries. ''Hi. About settled in?''

''Yes, actually, I am.''

Holding the door open, she let him precede her into the kitchen. Her skin tingled when he lightly brushed against her arm. She grabbed the last items and hurried in after him. ''Thanks for your help. Uh, just set those down on the table.''

He did so, then leaned against the counter, thumbs hooked in his pockets, and observed while she stored the foodstuffs like a busy ant during harvest. His observant manner made her nervous, and the cottage seemed smaller with his dynamic presence.

Like the construction workers next door, he wore no shirt, only jeans and sturdy work boots. His hair was mussed by the breeze, and his bronzed skin glistened in the August heat. His eyes reminded her of precious gemstones, polished to perfection so that their depths seemed endless. He was, quite simply, the most handsome man she'd ever met.

She wondered how she'd managed to work beside

him the past few days without getting tongue-tied and making a fool of herself. Well, work was one thing. They were both on their best professional behavior. Here, in the privacy of her new quarters, the atmosphere changed, becoming vibrant with expectation.

The kitchen, ample when she was alone, was much too confining with him there. She brushed his arm when she opened the refrigerator to put the milk away.

"Excuse me," she quickly said so he'd know it was an accident. Then she stumbled over his foot when she closed the fridge and tried to move away.

She caught the back of a chair before he could reach out to help, steadied herself, then rushed to the opposite side of the table and removed cans from a bag. Opening the cabinet beside the stove, she stored spices and cooking oil.

"Do you like to cook?" he asked, eyeing her purchases.

First she hesitated, then realized her reluctance to tell him anything about herself was silly. The question was innocent. "Yes. My mother is a wonderful cook, and she always let me help, so it's something I've always done."

"What does your father like to do?"

"Fish. Hunt. All the manly arts." She smiled, remembering her first fish.

"What?" Beau demanded.

"When I caught my first eating-size fish, I got so excited, I whipped the pole back over my head so hard the fish flew off. My mother was sitting up on the bank reading a book. The fish slapped her upside the head and fell into her lap on top of the book. Startled, she shrieked and flung both fish and book into the lake. I froze in horror, knowing I was in deep trouble.''

''Were you?''

''Well, there was this minute of silence, then my father cracked up. He laughed so hard he nearly fell in the lake. My mother joined in. I burst into tears.''

He looked surprised. ''Why?''

''I'd planned on catching our supper. Instead I lost my fish, hit my mom and ruined her book, which was slowly drifting out into the lake and turning soggy. I was eight years old and had pictured myself a heroine.''

While he chuckled and managed to look sympathetic at the same time, she opened the pantry and, standing on tiptoe, placed staples on the top shelf.

''Here, let me do that,'' he said.

Reaching over her shoulder, he took the can from her and deftly put it on the shelf. His torso pressed lightly against her back.

''Is this where you want it?'' he asked.

His voice vibrated through her like a wind chime in an ancient temple, deep and mysterious, a call to something just as enigmatic, just as alluring, deep within her.

She nodded, unable to speak, barely able to breathe.

One by one, he placed the canned goods in the upper cabinets until the bag was empty. All the while, she stood as if frozen, framed within the enclosure formed by his body and the counter, her heart pounding a doomsday knell.

"Is that all?" he asked.

"Yes," she whispered.

Neither moved, although she knew she should do something to break this strange spell. She couldn't. It had already grown too strong, wrapping around and around her like a golden cage formed of half-understood needs and longings she didn't want to recognize.

His hands settled on her upper arms. With the gentlest of touches, he caressed up and down. The awareness was so strong her flesh burned wherever he stroked, although he barely skimmed the surface of her skin.

"I want to kiss you," he murmured into her hair.

The golden cage shimmered and hummed around her.

"Kiss? I want to ravish you." He gave a half laugh and nuzzled her ear. "But Uncle Nick says men can't do that to women anymore."

She tried for sophisticated nonchalance. "Did he give you any hints on what you could do?"

"Yeah." His voice was a mere whisper of sound, silk rushing softly over silk, as he kissed the sensitive skin under her ear. Chills raced over her arms. "He said we had to go slow, that a woman must be won with gentleness so she wouldn't be afraid to come to a man.''

"Is that…is that…" She couldn't get past the breath caught in her throat.

"What I'm doing with you?" he finished for her. "Yes. I want to be gentle with you."

"So I'll come to you?" The words were wistful instead of sardonic, as she'd intended.

"Hold that thought," he whispered.

He gathered her hair into one hand and lifted it from her back, stripping the scrunchy band down its length. He followed the action with the incredibly soft caress of his breath as he blew against her neck.

She shivered delicately, anticipation building with each minute that ticked by. All the things she hadn't felt, hadn't *let* herself feel in years, came rushing back to her—the dizzy way a person could react when in the presence of that certain other, the childish glee that came with great happiness, the lightness that invaded the heart.

"Your skin is so soft," he murmured, skimming his fingers along her arms, then over the back of her neck, causing another shiver. "So warm."

But she was the one melting from his heat.

"Every time I see you I want to do this." He bent his head once more, this time letting his lips move over her.

That sweet, compelling need to lean against him had her clutching the counter edge to keep from doing it. Where was her control, her sense of self-preservation?

"But that isn't even half what I want to do, what we could do together…if we put our minds to it."

The suggestion was so sexy, so beguiling, so impossible to ignore. Liquid heat built inside her, turning her blood into a hot flow of honey. "But we won't," she managed to say. "We won't do anything foolish."

"Not now," he agreed, a brief respite. "But later, when things…change."

He caressed her arms again, sliding up and down in easy forays that had her all the more tense each time he passed her breasts without touching. She was burning for him to do more, even as she wondered what things had to change and why, when she was dying for him now.

"What things?" she asked, unable to stop.

"When you know me better," he said huskily, his lips against the side of her neck. "When we're lovers."

A coal of fire fell to the pit of her stomach and glowed brightly. "We won't be," she said desperately, not sure where the desperation came from.

"Then we'll wonder all our lives." He kissed her cheek, the corner of her mouth. "How it might have been." Her temple and the curve of her jaw. "How much we missed." Her collarbone, peeling the tank top and bra strap down her arm as he did. "How good it could be between us."

"But we'll never know." She sounded uncertain.

"Won't we?" he demanded in a low growl. "Won't we?"

He moved fractionally closer, his body touching hers all the way down her back, not harshly, not nearly as much as she craved, but enough...enough. She went all hot and totally unstrung inside.

"Can you deny this?" he asked.

He brushed lightly against her so that she knew exactly the strength of his desire. And her own.

"A physical attraction," she said, and laughed as if it was meaningless and less than nothing to her.

"Don't scoff. Kingdoms have fallen over less," he advised with a certain wry humor.

Clasping her wrists, he tugged her free of the counter and crossed their arms at her waist. His powerful forearms pressed against the undersides of her breasts. She felt her nipples contract with painful quickness. One large warm hand kneaded her abdomen, stirring more sensation there.

"This must stop," she told him sternly, seeking reason, wanting anger so she could push him away.

"Why, when it feels so good?"

She moved her head restlessly, refusing his wandering kisses. The pleasurable moistness of his lips against her skin made her long for deeper, wilder kisses from him.

"I could touch you until I'm weak from it," he told her, pressing his cheek to her temple, locking her more tightly into his arms and swaying gently to and fro. "I want to taste you…here and here and here."

He nibbled her ear, her cheek, her mouth.

"I want to be in you."

She gasped at the raw need in his voice.

"I want to be in you so deep, neither of us will know where one ends and the other begins. That's how it is for me when I'm around you."

"But you've been distant at the office all week."

"Because I didn't dare be anything else."

He laughed with barely a sound. She felt the movement of his chest against her. Leaning into his strength, she laid her head on his shoulder and let his lips roam where they would. The shimmering golden cage merged with the honey flow of hunger so that she was filled and surrounded, inside and out, as if he touched her everywhere, even her most secret places.

She sighed and closed her eyes.

"Shh," he said. "Shh."

"I want…I ache…" She heard the despair. Wanting and aching and loving led to heartbreak. She knew it, knew it and didn't care, not at this moment.

He turned her face to his and kissed her full on the mouth, a long, lingering kiss that melded passion with passion into one bright conflagration. At last he lifted his head and eased away a tiny bit.

"It'll be there for us," he said, as if he, too, were shaken by the fierceness between them. "When we're ready. When the time comes."

He chuckled, bringing a measure of sanity to the moment. She blinked, then turned as he gave her room. No words came to her, either to demand that he stay or go.

"And when it does come, there'll be an explosion. I wonder if we'll ever recover."

With that, he swung around and departed. All the beautiful golden brightness went with him. What she had thought was a cage had been an illusion, one of her own making, she realized.

Desire between a man and a woman could be a powerful thing, but she'd never known it could wrap all around and inside a person until nothing else existed.

She touched her lips. They felt warm, as fragile as a baby's first breath.

Shelby dressed in a light summer suit and drove the short distance to a charming little church on the west side of town. The church was perched on the flat top of a hillock with a carpet of smoothly mown lawn sweeping down to the main road. The white spire and rosette window of stained glass over the door reminded her of home and the church she'd attended all her life.

After parking between two SUVs, which made her subcompact station wagon look like something that had shrunk in the wash, she approached the entrance. She almost stopped, turned and ran before she got there.

Daltons filled the portico, talking and laughing with the minister and four other people. One spotted her and met her on the steps. Beau took her hand and tucked it in the crook of his elbow.

"Come on," he said. "You're just in time to meet the whole kit and caboodle."

"I, well, perhaps we should go inside. The service begins at eleven."

"Nah. The preacher's here. They can't start without him. Uncle Nick, here's the nurse I mentioned."

To her consternation, she was tugged up the steps and into the midst of the group. An older gentleman, his hair white, but with those incredible Dalton eyes, smiled at her.

She would have known he was the family patriarch even without the introduction. Beau's uncle was tall, lanky and broad-shouldered. He had the same facial bone structure of strong planes and hollows but in a face that was thinner than those of the nephews and showed the lines of both laughter and sadness in a life long lived. She guessed he was around seventy.

"Glad to meet you," she murmured.

"Same here." He took her hand and held it while gazing at her. His smile was gentle. "I'm glad my nephew finally found someone to help him in the office. He told me about your working together."

Shelby wasn't sure what that meant, so she nodded and held on to her smile. Little eddies of panic—she didn't know where from—swirled through her. Beau stepped closer and clasped her arm. She at once felt comforted.

"This is Pastor Betters. The twins, you know," he said, continuing the introductions. He gestured to another woman. "This is Alison Harvey, Travis's fiancée. I think you've met Zack and Honey."

She nodded to the pastor and the couples.

"These two are the rest of the Daltons—Roni and Seth, my siblings. They both live in Boise."

Roni was a petite brunette with the Dalton eyes surrounded by long black lashes. The combination was so lovely, it was difficult not to stare.

Shelby blinked at Seth. He was a couple of inches shorter than the other Dalton males, but had a powerful build. He also had black hair and the darkest eyes she'd ever seen. Latino, she decided. Or Native American.

His smile flashed brilliantly. "I'm the dark horse in the family," he told her.

"He's the family attorney and financial wizard," Beau said. "He keeps us on the right side of the tax laws and all that. Roni writes learning tools for kids for a computer educational company. Those two got the brains in the family."

"Hey, I'm pretty smart," Trevor protested. He gave her a wicked smile. "Smart enough to recognize a good thing when I see it. Come sit by me. We'll share a hymnal."

He gave her a hopeful leer that brought laughter

from his family. Beau stepped between them. "Sorry, cuz, but she's with me."

"Come in," the pastor invited, holding the door open. "The organist has played the same song twice, a sign she's getting impatient with me."

Shelby found herself seated between Beau and his uncle on a long pew filled with Daltons. Eyes bored into the back of her head and she felt very much on display. The next hour passed in a haze while she conscientiously tried to concentrate on the sermon.

To her surprise, Marta, who cooked the delicious pastries at the B and B, was the organist. They smiled at each other at the end of the service.

Once more outside, Shelby felt a bit surrounded as the family stayed close to her.

"Beau, why don't you bring Shelby out to the ranch?" his uncle suggested. "She can have lunch with us."

Beau's sister pressed forward. "Do come," she urged. "Otherwise the women are outnumbered."

Trevor mussed her hair. "Huh. I've never seen any guys who could stand up to you."

Roni ignored him. "I'll ride with you and show you the way," she said.

Before Shelby could think up a good reason to refuse, she found herself in the car, the female Dalton in the passenger seat and giving directions on getting to the Dalton ranch. It was a forty minute drive.

At the end of the gravel ranch road, Shelby drove under a huge log supported by two others. "The

Seven Devils Ranch, 1865,'' she read the words burned into the log. ''Your relatives came west shortly after the Civil War.''

''Yes, they were from Tennessee.''

''My mother was from Kentucky, a small town near the Tennessee border.''

''We're probably kin,'' Roni joked. ''You have the Dalton eyes. Our ancestress who came west had red hair. Park there by the horse rail in front of the house.''

Shelby did as told. Uncle Nick rode with Beau, she noticed. They both glanced at her when they got out. Beau held the door open to the ranch house, which had a log-constructed central part and wood framing on the two wings to each side of the center.

''Welcome,'' he murmured as she passed him.

Her heart thundered as they went into the large living room. A comfortable leather sofa and various chairs invited casual lounging. One wall held a TV and lots of books.

Beyond the living room was a big kitchen with a dining room to the left of that. She thought there must be at least six bedrooms divided between the two wings.

''I'll give you a tour while the men get dinner on the table,'' Roni volunteered.

Shelby caught the scowl Beau directed at his sister, then his quick smile as he followed his uncle into the kitchen. She went with Roni to inspect the house.

It was larger than it first appeared. At the end of

one wing was a large bedroom with a bathroom and sitting area that ran the depth of the house. "Uncle Nick's room," Roni said. "This was the nursery."

The nursery was a very small room next to a bathroom. There was another nice-size bedroom and a smaller one.

"Tink, Uncle Nick's daughter, had the nursery," Beau's sister continued. "She disappeared when she was three or so."

"Disappeared?" Shelby said.

"At the scene of an auto accident. Her mother died in the crash, but Tink just disappeared."

"She was never found?"

"No. It was terrible for Uncle Nick, losing his own wife and daughter like that, then having a bunch of orphans to raise on top of it all. He was wonderful to us."

Shelby clenched her teeth as the pain of losing a child rushed over her with the chilling suddenness of a dam breaking. The tears pressed behind her eyes. Memories played tug-of-war with her heart as she glanced into the empty room that had once been the nursery of a beloved child.

"Seth, as the oldest, had the big bedroom in this wing. Zack had the smaller one." She led the way to the other wing. "The twins shared this bedroom while Beau had one to himself. The other was for guests. I had the rose room."

They peeked in the open door of the rose room,

another large bedroom that ran the depth of the house on the west end and had its own sitting area.

"It's really charming," Shelby said, admiring the room with its rosy tones and floral wallpaper, a large bed and a rocking chair with a table and lamp nearby.

"Zack and Honey use it now that they're married. Travis and Alison are working on their house over in the woods." Roni gestured toward the front of the house. "Ah, there's Janis and Keith. Janis is Alison's sister. Keith owns the next ranch over the ridge north of here."

With all these names and relationships whirling through her head, Shelby trailed after Roni as they went to greet the new arrivals. At the door, her heart stopped as she watched the couple come up the walk.

They had a baby. A very young baby.

Beau's arm settled across her shoulders. "This is the last bunch you'll meet today, I promise," he murmured as if detecting the tremor that rushed through her.

The desperation welled in her. "Perhaps I should return to town."

"There's plenty of food and picnic tables outside where we can eat."

A flurry ensued with the arrival of the other couple. Introductions were made, then everyone was invited to grab a plate, fill it and eat wherever they wanted.

The three couples, plus Trevor, Roni and Beau, sweeping Shelby along with him, elected to head for the shade under an oak tree while Seth stayed inside to talk to his uncle about ranch business.

Roni rolled her eyes. "Whoever gets Seth will have to surgically remove him from his work first."

Janis, placing the sleeping baby in an infant carrier, spoke up. "We need to find someone for him. And you," she added. "You and Seth and Trevor are the only ones left."

"What about me?" Trevor demanded, hearing his name.

"No woman in her right mind would take you on," Roni informed him with a mock-sad expression.

The cousins solemnly agreed.

"Huh," the twin snorted. "Shelby isn't spoken for." He waggled his eyebrows across the table at her.

"Who says?" Beau asked in a lazy, assured tone with a hint of challenge.

Several pairs of eyes studied him, then her. Shelby felt the heat go right up to her hairline.

"See what you've done," Beau said to Trev. "You're embarrassing my date."

"I'm not your date," Shelby protested, feeling as if she had fallen down the rabbit hole and landed at the Mad Hatter's tea party.

"That's right," Roni said. "She's my friend and she came with me." She glanced at Alison and Travis. "How's the house coming?"

"Great," Travis said. "The countertops will be finished this week, and all will be ready for the big moment."

"They're getting married next weekend," Roni explained.

"Oh. Congratulations," Shelby said sincerely.

Beau reached for the salt and pepper shakers, his thigh touching hers as he did. When he finished and replaced them in the center of the table, he was closer, his leg still lightly touching hers as they ate the meal of oven-fried chicken, potatoes, green beans and a bowl of mixed melons and strawberries.

Alison smiled at her. "The ceremony is Saturday afternoon at my parents' home in the city. We're having a dinner reception here that evening for those who can't make the other. We would love to have you come."

"That's very nice of you…" Shelby began.

"She would love to attend the dinner," Beau said before she could frame a tactful refusal. "With me," he added as Trevor opened his mouth.

"I wouldn't want to intrude," she said.

"You won't be," he assured her with the typical disregard men showed toward the logistics of planning a big event such as this.

"Really," Alison said, "you must come."

Shelby nodded, not sure how to refuse in the face of all the welcoming smiles around the table. The other women talked about the plans, and Shelby realized her acceptance was taken for granted when Alison asked her if she would mind tending the punch bowl.

"I would be honored."

"Good girl," Beau murmured for her ears alone.

Looking up, her eyes met those of Trevor. He winked at her in his good-natured way. She smiled, then when no one was paying attention, sighed rather shakily as she felt herself becoming entangled in the Dalton clan. They were very much like her family at home.

The baby gave a whimper at that moment.

"Junior wants his lunch," the young mother announced.

Although neither wore rings, Shelby assumed the parents were married. She looked at her plate while Keith handed the child to his wife, who turned her back to the group and nursed the infant.

A sharp, hot pain went through her breasts as memories flooded through her. For a moment she could see the blue of her own baby's eyes gazing up at her in complete trust as the tiny mouth took nourishment from her body.

That sweet, innocent gaze. The tiny fingers clutching at her blouse. The rosebud lips moving against her.

The ache intensified as the baby across the table made suckling noises. A tremor raced over her. She couldn't swallow or speak or breathe for a moment.

An arm slipped around her waist. Warmth and strength flowed over and into her as Beau held her. She was able to release the breath knotted in her throat and cast him a glance of gratitude.

He watched her solemnly for a second, his eyes fathoms deep. ''Okay?'' he asked almost silently.

Nodding, she whispered, ''It was just...'' She couldn't think of an explanation.

His glance went to Janis and the baby, then back to her. ''Someday you'll tell me.'' His eyes locked with hers.

She shook her head slightly. Other than her parents, she had never spoken of those dark, angry, hurtful days, not to anyone.

''Someday,'' he said.

Chapter Five

Shelby returned to the medical office after lunch on Monday. Getting out of her car, which she'd parked at the rear of the lot, she spied Beau sitting in an old-fashioned yard swing under an arbor of rose vines.

"Hi," he called. "Care to join me while I finish my lunch?"

She crossed the grass and stood in front of him, uncertain about sitting on the two-person swing. He moved over, indicating she should sit. She did so reluctantly.

"I won't bite," he murmured, giving her a wicked smile, then taking a chunk out of his sandwich. "What are you doing back here?"

"I thought I would work on the old files in the

attic this afternoon. School doesn't start until next Monday, so I'll have the afternoons free this week.''

He frowned. Sure he was going to refuse, her heart dropped to her stomach while she tried to think of a reason she had to start right away.

"It'll be hot up there," he warned, "too hot to work in the afternoons."

"I don't mind the heat."

"I know Miss Pickford is a slave driver, but even she won't expect you to chance a stroke for the Historical Society. How about I hook up a fan and we work for a couple of hours after dinner each night?"

"I'd like to start now," she said doggedly. "I don't have anything to do."

He finished the sandwich. "You could help me out in the afternoons."

"I don't want to be tired when school starts," she quickly said, then realized how lame that sounded.

"Right. Working in a hundred-degree attic every afternoon is a dip in the lake compared to an air-conditioned office."

"But I could work at my own pace," she reminded him.

He threw up his hands in surrender. "Do as you please. Women always do," he added darkly.

She couldn't help it. She laughed.

After a minute, he did, too.

Still smiling, he offered her a drink of his lemon-ade. She took a sip and handed the glass back. He drained it and stood. "Time for me to get back to work. Have you seen my place?"

"No. I thought you lived at the ranch."

"I'm staying in the little house back here. Come on. I'll give you the grand tour."

Carrying his plate and glass, he led the way to the white cabin that was similar in style to the big house where his office was located, but on a much smaller scale.

"It's one room," he told her, holding the door open.

She stepped inside. "It's like a dollhouse."

There was about six feet of counter space along the back wall between two windows. A tiny refrigerator, stove and sink were snugly fitted into the counters.

A dark pine daybed divided the kitchen from the living room. Shelves held a television, books and medical magazines. There were two chairs pushed up to a white table at a side wall, forming the dining area. A screened porch ran across the backside of the house.

"Closet," he said, pointing to double doors. "Bath." He pointed to one other door.

"It's very...compact," she finished, trying to think of a polite word.

He washed his plate and glass, leaving them on a rack to dry. "This was the caretaker's place in olden days. The kitchen was added when Dr. Barony's mother moved in, then his son lived out here while he decided what he wanted to be when he finished growing up.''

''What did he decide?''

''Last I heard, he went off to discover himself or the world and never came back.''

Had he left a wife or lover and child behind? ''Was he married?'' she asked.

''Not that I ever knew.'' Beau glanced at his watch. ''Sorry, but I've got to run.'' They strolled over to the big house. ''There're records in two of the bedrooms on the second floor,'' he told her as they entered the office. ''Start on those. I'll rig up a fan for the attic on Wednesday.''

Beau immediately went to his office while she climbed the stairs to the second floor. It was actually cool up here, probably due to the air-conditioning on the floor below, but to her, it was the chill of loneliness that attached to old, empty houses that had once known the busy happiness of family life.

She shivered slightly as the cold air swirled around her when she opened a door off the hall. As promised, the bedroom contained file boxes of records, each labeled with beginning and ending dates. She realized these boxes were the last three years of the old doctor's practice.

The overhead light came on when she flicked the wall switch. With the yellowed window shades raised, she had sufficient light to work.

Fishing index cards and a pen out of her purse, she sat on the floor and began listing names, birthdays and deaths. As she became absorbed in the town's history through its citizens, she lost all track of time.

"Hey," a masculine voice called from the stairs.

Startled, Shelby jerked her head up from the folder she was studying. A woman had surprised the doctor and her husband by giving birth to triplets, something that occurred naturally only once in about two hundred thousand births.

"Dinner is served," Beau announced from the door. "Interesting stuff?"

She closed the folder and stuck it partway in the file to mark the spot. "A woman had triplets."

"That would have been the Bronson girls."

"Yes. Did you know them?"

"I knew the parents. They moved out of the state shortly after the kids were born. One of the girls died of SIDS later that year, we heard."

Sudden infant death syndrome, Shelby translated. She knew the unbearable pain of loss, the disbelief and anger, the terrible helplessness they must have felt.

"A lot of marriages don't withstand the loss of a child," she murmured.

"I think theirs did." He spoke quietly, as if he understood her grief.

She nodded, then stood, arranged her notes in a neat stack, grabbed her purse and headed for the door.

"Dinner's at my place," he said, flicking out the light.

"Did you cook?" she asked, striving for a lighter note.

"Well..." he began modestly, then grinned. "I sent out for pizza, Hawaiian style with ham and pineapple. Okay?"

Her hesitation wasn't with his choice but with the wisdom of being alone with him at the cabin. Outside, she found the shadows had grown long upon the lawn while she'd read through nearly two years of records.

"This way," he said.

Without giving her time to reconsider, he took her arm and coaxed her into his place. The scent of hot cheese and tomato sauce made her mouth water. She realized it had been seven hours since lunch.

"Yeah, it's late," he said when she glanced at her watch in surprise. "You're a hard worker."

"Not really. I just become absorbed." She laid her purse on the wicker table next to the daybed and held up her hands. "I need to wash the dust off."

Entering the door he'd pointed out earlier, she found a snug but complete bathroom with tub, sink and toilet. A shower was rigged up on the claw-foot tub, and a chrome shower rail encircled it. A blue curtain was pushed to one end.

An electric toothbrush was located on a small shelf attached to the wall. His razor was propped on its edge on the sink. She was careful not to disturb it when she washed her hands and splashed cool water on her face. Once clean and refreshed, she returned to the all-purpose living room.

"Out here," he called.

She followed his voice to the porch. Paper plates, napkins and the pizza were on a white wicker coffee table. Glasses of ice and soda were on the end table. He sat on the two-seater wicker sofa. She chose the matching rocking chair. It creaked in a friendly fashion under her weight.

He handed her a plate. "Help yourself."

"Thanks."

It was peaceful out here. Crickets chirped. Birds sang evening songs from the nearby forest. An occasional car droned down the street.

"Are you going to fix up the second floor of the big house as a residence?" she asked, feeling they should talk about work or things related to work.

"I hadn't planned on it."

She nodded. "The cabin is charming."

"And big enough for a bachelor," he added.

"Yes."

"But it wouldn't work for a family."

"No," she agreed.

In the ensuing silence, she ate and tried to think of something else to say, something innocuous that wouldn't lead to family and things she didn't want to discuss.

"Find anything interesting today?" he asked.

She felt his gaze probing her expression. Shaking her head, she stubbornly ate and pretended not to notice. What did he suspect?

"Except the triplets," he said.

"Oh, yes. That was interesting. Were they among the founding families?"

"No. The husband arrived with a logging company and stayed only as long as it was here. When the company moved on, he and his family did, too."

"Mmm," she said. While triplets were interesting, that family wasn't hers. She needed to get to the attic to see if the old records went back thirty years. Her scalp tingled all at once, as if she'd been touched by a ghost.

Would she find her birth family here, or was this a wild-goose chase, as her father had warned?

Looking up, she encountered heavenly blue eyes that seemed to see clear to her soul. She tried to smile, but it was impossible.

"What is it about you?" he murmured. "What is it?"

She couldn't think of a thing to say, so she ducked her head and forced the rest of the pizza down. As soon as possible, she fled that probing gaze that seemed to know she was there for other purposes.

He walked her to the car, his eyes narrowed against the last fading rays of the sun. Undisclosed thoughts filtered through that thoughtful gaze, making her nervous. She quickly drove off.

Beau kept an eye on the house next door as he worked on the resort with his family the following Wednesday. He wanted to catch Shelby when she returned from her workout.

"Ready?" Seth asked.

He got back to business when his brother spoke. They lifted a wall frame and nailed it into place. Seth was the oldest of the Dalton orphans and the most serious. As an attorney and a certified financial planner, he had the sharpest mind of any man Beau had ever met. Seth was also a good carpenter, who, like himself, had paid his own way through college by working summers in construction.

Catching movement along the lake path, Beau quickly checked it out. Shelby, her lithe body sleek with sweat from an hour-long jog, was heading for the cottage. He was glad he'd worn underwear as his body hardened in response.

"Your new nurse is good-looking. The buzz about her has reached every bachelor in the county, it seems," Seth said, obviously amused by the interest.

Beau watched as Shelby entered the house next door. "There's a mystery about her. I checked her credentials. She was a top-notch pediatrics nurse in her hometown, even got an award from the mayor for saving a bunch of lives during an emergency. Why would she leave that for a part-time job in a place fifty miles from nowhere?"

Seth considered the situation. "Maybe you had better find out."

"That's what I thought." Beau tossed a grin toward his brother. "There is a slight problem, though. I tend to forget the questions when I'm with her."

"I think I noticed the sparks Sunday when she came out to the ranch."

"I've never been so hot for a woman," Beau admitted to this quiet Dalton. Seth could be as silent as the grave when he chose. Any confidences shared with him were respected.

"I take it you're over Julie."

The statement sounded innocent, but Beau knew his lawyer brother rarely made idle comments. "I never—" he began, then stopped at the futile lie.

Julie had been Travis's wife. The couple had met in first grade and been in love all their lives. She'd died in childbirth over two years ago. Travis had gone off into the woods for a long time until he could live with the guilt and the grief.

Since no one had known of his feelings, Beau'd had to keep his pain hidden. Obviously he hadn't done as well at concealment as he'd thought.

"Yeah, I got over her," he said softly, hearing the echo of sorrow even as he said the words. "I didn't know anyone knew." His snort of laughter rang hollow. "I guess everyone did."

"Trevor mentioned it to me," Seth said. "He was more than half in love with her, too. She was a beautiful woman, in spirit as well as in person. I'm glad Travis found Alison before bitterness took over his life." His dark eyes surveyed the cottage. "I like your nurse. She would make a good wife for a small-town doc."

Beau hammered a brace into place to support the

new wall until they got the others up. "You're as bad as Uncle Nick. He gave me his seal of approval, too."

Seth grinned. "Next he'll be telling her to seduce you. He figures we're all honorable men and will do the right thing by marrying the woman we're sleeping with."

"Hey, what happened to you and that blonde I saw you with last month before I left town?" Beau asked, striving for a lighter tone.

"Nothing. She found a richer catch and moved on."

"I can tell your heart was broken," Beau said dryly.

"Yeah. Fortunately, I heal fast," Seth assured his younger brother.

Laughing, they got back to work. When the three outer walls were finished, they called it a day. The twins had gone home an hour ago. After Seth headed for the ranch, Beau walked across the grass to the house next door.

On the way, he was aware of his heart speeding up and the heavy throb of blood through his body. Both amused and exasperated by the response, he reminded his libido that he was a thirty-year-old man, not a boy driven by the whims of his body.

Like his place, the cottage had a back porch, this one facing the lake. He lifted his hand to knock on the screen door, then paused when he heard Shelby's voice. Surprised, he concluded she had company and wondered who it was.

"Mom?" he heard her say. "Yes, they got the phone hooked up today. I wanted to give you the number."

Ah, she was on the telephone, reporting in to her folks. He smiled as he deduced her parents were probably a lot like his uncle in their expectations.

He listened shamelessly as Shelby explained her change in jobs from high school teaching to working in his office on her free days. As she told an amusing story about Ruth and Bertie, he found himself nodding and smiling. The humor disappeared at her next words.

"No," she said, "I haven't found out anything about that yet. I've joined the Historical Society, though, and have access to several years' medical records, so I think it's only a matter of time. Yes, I'm being very careful."

Her voice faded as she left the kitchen area. Beau quietly left the porch and returned to the building site.

Suspicion gnawed at him as he drove to his temporary home behind the clinic. Shelby didn't know she was occupying the house he'd intended to live in while working on the lodge. Later, he'd planned to enlarge the cottage into a home for a family. If he ever had one.

Inside the caretaker's cabin, he tossed off his clothing and stepped into the shower. While he shampooed and washed up, he kept coming up with questions.

What was she trying to find out? Why did she think the old medical records would give her the answer?

Why did she need to be careful? Was there danger in her quest?

If Shelby was delving into something she shouldn't, maybe he'd better stay close and be on guard for her safety.

A sardonic chuckle escaped him. Uncle Nick would approve the sentiment. He still thought men were supposed to protect women. Tell that to the modern female.

While Shelby might not be *his* woman, still, there was something between them. Besides, he liked the idea of watching out for her. Finished with the shower, he wrapped a towel around his hips, checked with information, then dialed her new number. The line was still busy.

"There's no danger, Dad," Shelby assured her father. "I'm just checking old records left by the doctor who used to practice here. No one's suspicious about my being in town or working at the clinic. After all, I am a nurse."

"This Dalton child," her father said in worried tones. "Someone might think there's a connection to you, that it could be you."

Shelby wished she hadn't told her folks so much about her boss and his family. "She disappeared when she was three years old. I was three days old when you and Mom picked me up from the hospital. Besides, no one knows I'm adopted, so no one would see a connection."

"Well, I don't like it. These small towns look after their own if they think someone's being threatened."

Shelby rolled her eyes. "Like another small town I could name?" she teased.

"Just be careful," he advised. "Here's your mother again."

"Shelby?"

"I'm here."

"Uh, I have some news."

Shelby knew by the tone that it wasn't good. "Yes?"

"Brent was in last weekend. He's, uh, married."

Funny, but her heart didn't lurch even a little bit at hearing her ex-husband's name. "Well, his parents still live there. I'm sure he wanted them to meet his bride."

"They've been married a couple of years," her mom continued. "They…they have a baby, a girl."

Shelby closed her eyes and willed the news not to hurt. She forced herself to accept it as she would information about someone she'd once known but who was distant from her world now. There was one thing she had to know. "The baby, is she okay?"

"She's fine. Normal."

"Then I'm glad for him. I really mean that."

Her mother's sigh was audible. "I didn't want to tell you, but I didn't want one of your friends mentioning it first. Sue was worried…"

Sue had been Shelby's mother-in-law. She still lived next door to her parents and was still their life-long friend. "Tell her not to be. I'm okay. Really. Brent and I both had a lot of growing up to do. I think we've managed to make it."

"Good. Your father and I love you very much, darling. Take care of yourself," her mother ordered in a slightly choked voice.

Shelby felt their love reach out to her over the miles to surround her like a protective aura. "I love you, too. Don't worry. I'm going to be fine. I promise."

"We'll hold you to that. Maybe you'll come home with a nice young man in tow."

Shelby started to laugh, but a vision of dark hair and blue eyes sprang into her mind. "Right," she said. "Prince Charming is surely just around the corner."

After she said goodbye, she sat in the chair and stared out at the long, narrow lake. Maybe it *was* good that she'd come to Lost Valley. Maybe here she'd end her quest and find a whole new life.

"Maybe," she said out loud, as if experimenting with a new word. "Maybe…"

Chapter Six

Shelby stared into the closet for a long time before finally pulling out a gauzy dress of deep gold with white and blue flowers printed along the hemline. It had its own white slip. With white sandals and matching purse, she thought she would be okay for the reception at the ranch.

At work that morning, Beau had reminded her of the event and volunteered to pick her up. Glancing at the clock, she hurried with dressing and makeup so she wouldn't keep him waiting.

Outside, she heard a car, then silence as the engine was turned off. Her heart went into overdrive.

"Ready?" Beau called from the open front door.

"Just about." She slipped into the sandals and grabbed some tissues, stuffing them into her purse.

One last glance in the mirror told her she was as ready as she would ever be. She joined him on the porch, locked the door and was ready. For some reason, this felt like an adventure of the first order.

"Where's the truck?" she asked, seeing a strange vehicle in the drive.

"At the ranch. Uncle Nick thought I should use the ranch wagon to bring my guest. He said the pickup wasn't dignified for a date."

"This isn't a date," she quickly corrected.

"Tell that to my uncle," he suggested wryly.

He held the door for her, saw her safely tucked inside, then got into the driver's seat. He paused before cranking up the engine. "You're beautiful."

"Thank you." She tried to sound modest but casual, as if she didn't take the compliment seriously. Her voice came out a husky croak.

"Really beautiful."

She glanced at him and wished she hadn't. His eyes devoured her on the spot. "Please don't," she said.

"Sorry. It's just…" He shrugged as if to say there were no words to explain the attraction.

Shaking his head, he started the sparkling clean station wagon and drove the miles to the Seven Devils Ranch with little conversation. Shelby was overwhelmed when she saw the crowd.

A white tent had been put up on the lawn. Under its shade, tables were covered in linen while the chairs were adorned with garlands of gaily colored ribbons.

A large table at one end held a huge tiered cake and bouquets of flowers.

Easels held digital pictures of the bridal pair and the wedding that had taken place that afternoon at the bride's home. The couple looked radiantly happy.

"Looks like everyone in the county is here," Beau said.

She realized she should have expected it since the Daltons had lived there for generations. Just as in her hometown, everyone turned out for weddings and funerals.

The new bride spotted her and Beau. Alison introduced her parents—her father was a U.S. senator—to the couple, then led her inside the ranch house while Beau chatted with the older couple.

"Uncle Nick is making the punch," she explained. "He says you're to help."

"I'd be glad to. Your outfit is lovely," Shelby said, following Alison to the large kitchen. The bride wore a blue silk dress with a lace jacket. An orchid was pinned to her shoulder.

"Thanks. My mom calls it my 'going-away' suit, but we're only going to walk through the woods to the other house after the reception, so it seems rather odd."

"Nothing wrong with observing tradition," Uncle Nick said, overhearing this last part. He smiled at Shelby. "Glad you could make it. Taste this punch and see what you think. We'll add champagne when we get it to the tent."

Shelby sipped a small glass of punch and pronounced it "delicious."

Alison was heralded by her new husband and dashed out to greet more guests. Shelby sensed a deep contentment in the quieter of the twins. Happiness will do that, she thought. From Amelia at the B and B, she knew he'd been married and lost his wife and child during birth.

A pang went through her at his loss and she sighed.

"You like working with Beau?" the uncle asked, his blue eyes delving into her innermost spirit just the way his nephew's did.

"Yes. Ruth and Bertie are wonderful, and everyone in town has been very kind."

He snorted as if this news neither surprised nor interested him. "The boy's taken a shine to you," he continued. "Being a doctor can be hard on a person. He needs a wife to welcome him home at night, someone who can comfort him when he needs it. Being a nurse and all, you would understand the stress."

It sounded as if Beau's uncle had decided she was the most likely candidate for the helpmate position. She got out a strangled sound that was meant to be a protest.

"Sometimes," the older man confided in a low tone, "a man doesn't see what's under his nose. You might need to seduce him."

"Uh-nn," she managed to croak before her throat closed up entirely.

"Good," he said as if she'd agreed wholeheartedly.

"I've seen the way he looks at you. It won't be any trouble." With a happy smile, he handed her a ring mold. "Here, Roni made this ice thing and said we had to use it. Tell Beau to come get the punch."

Shelby fled the homey kitchen before she passed out. It was only when she was outside that she was able to breathe comfortably again. She dodged through the crowd, removed the ice ring, which appeared to be punch with fruit frozen inside, from the mold and placed it in the crystal punch bowl.

"Hi." A familiar voice spoke behind her. "Uncle Nick has put you to work, I see."

"Uh, yes," she said to Beau.

His eyes narrowed and he leaned closer to study her face as she told him his uncle needed him. She couldn't look him in the eye.

"Your face was red when you came tearing out of the house. Did Uncle Nick tell you to seduce me?"

The heat rushed to her head once more, making her dizzy. "Of course not." It came out weakly.

"The old codger," Beau said with an affectionate chuckle. "He tells that to every eligible female who comes on the place. He had a heart attack back in the spring. He's afraid he's not going to get us all settled in with a family before he kicks the bucket."

"Maybe he thinks, without him here, you'll need a wife to keep you in line," she said, recovering her poise.

"He's probably right," Beau agreed good-naturedly. He held the screen door open so she could precede him into the house. "Hey, Uncle Nick, would you explain again to Shelby about seducing me? She doesn't seem to have caught on yet."

"Young smart-mouth," his uncle scolded.

"Uncle Nick, it's time to dress," Roni said.

The older man hurried from the kitchen at a glance from his niece.

Roni thrust gallon jugs of punch into Beau's hands and handed a stack of crystal plates to Shelby. "Shelby can seduce you on her own time. Right now, I need help. Seth said we should have hired a caterer. Perhaps he was right."

"No, he wasn't," Beau said. "It would make folks uncomfortable to have waiters pussyfooting around."

"Well, I'm sure Alison's family is used to better things," his sister informed him. She arranged fruit on a platter, her hands trembling slightly.

"Everything looks wonderful," Alison hastened to assure the other woman, who wasn't quite as self-confident as Shelby had assumed. "Did you make the cake, too?"

"Heavens, no. Marta from the B and B did it." Roni rushed across the kitchen to the refrigerator, grabbed another bowl of fruit and continued with her chore. "As soon as Uncle Nick is ready, we'll do toasts, then cut the cake, then eat. Beau, all you guys are expected to propose toasts to the couple. Get everyone herded up."

Beau looked pained, but nodded. He gestured for

Shelby to follow him out. She worked on setting up the food table while he went to round up his relatives.

In a few minutes, Beau had the male Daltons in tow. The groom, bride and her parents accompanied the group. Roni and her uncle came out of the house, each carrying a food tray, and joined Shelby in the tent. After the platters were in place, the formal reception was announced.

The minister from the local church said a blessing for the couple and spoke briefly on the sanctity of marriage.

After the guests had glasses of punch, champagne or a combination, Seth started the toast by wishing Alison and Travis an abundance of happiness, with a smidgen of trouble so they would know the difference.

The crowd laughed, cheered and sipped their drink.

Like the good fairies at Sleeping Beauty's birthday celebration, each cousin added to the toast. Health, wealth and long life were mentioned by Zack, Trevor and Beau.

When Alison's father was pressed to give advice, he told the couple to "never let the sun set on a quarrel."

Finally, Roni held up her glass. "And may all your troubles be little ones." She pretended to cradle a baby and rock it in her arms.

Beau, his gaze irresistibly drawn to Shelby, was surprised as an odd expression flitted over her face before she, too, smiled and took a sip from her glass.

He'd have sworn that, for the briefest second, he'd seen despair in her eyes. Hmm, another part of the mystery of her.

When Roni shepherded the wedded pair behind the table for the ceremonial cutting of the cake, he made his way to Shelby's side.

The day was pleasant, in the high seventies, and the breeze brought her scent to him—a light fragrance that teased his senses with images of a floral bower and a soft, mossy bed.

He was brought back to the present when Alison said she had a surprise announcement. "My favorite sister and her most significant other are going to tie the knot today. They were going to wait until our festivities were over, but it seems appropriate that their happiness be added to ours. Janis, Keith, is now okay?"

The couple next to him looked at each other and nodded. They started forward. "Can you watch the baby?" Janis asked, holding the bundle out to Shelby.

Beau saw surprise and something like alarm spread over her face before she took the baby, which was only a couple of months old. With anyone else, he would have assumed she wasn't familiar with babies and was scared of dropping the little one, but Shelby was a pediatric nurse.

The baby roused at being jostled from sleep and would have protested with a cry, but Shelby gently bounced the child. The infant immediately settled into slumber again.

When he looked into her eyes, he realized his earlier assessment had been close to the mark. There was despair or some equally intense emotion in those depths. Without pausing to think, he wrapped his arms around her and the baby, lending his comfort to whatever was bothering her.

During the brief ceremony, Beau continued to hold Shelby and the tiny bundle. She felt exactly right in his arms. Even the baby didn't seem out of place.

He frowned, trying to think it through. All his adult life had been focused on getting his medical training, paying off his college loans and someday opening a practice here in his hometown. Except for a very brief entanglement nearly six years ago, he'd never had a serious involvement with anyone.

The memory of the short vacation produced an uncomfortable sense of shame and regret. He'd used the woman to assuage his own pain when Julie had married Travis. The woman, a classmate he'd run into at their reunion, had used him for a similar reason. They'd been two lost souls who briefly found comfort with each other, then moved on.

As the minister pronounced Janis and Keith husband and wife, the baby puckered up. Beau smiled when Shelby inserted her pinkie finger into the tiny mouth before a wail could erupt. The infant latched on and nursed contentedly.

''You may kiss the bride,'' the minister said.

Applause broke out as the groom did so.

The senator held up his hands for quiet. "I propose a toast," he said.

Everyone held their glasses ready.

"To my daughters." He motioned to Alison and Janis. "And two new sons-in-law." He nodded to Travis and Keith. "However, I request that you consider your ol' dad's heart when planning future surprises like double weddings."

He laid a hand over his heart, which elicited laughter from the wedding guests.

Beau took a sip of champagne punch, then held his glass so Shelby, too, could drink to the toast.

"This younger generation is hard on us older ones," Mr. Harvey continued with a wry smile. "So I'd like to toast my lovely wife, who can manage a thousand details while I'm still trying to find a pencil to start a list."

Beau chuckled. He again shared his glass with Shelby.

"A final toast," Mr. Harvey said. "To a man whose heart is as big as the land he loves, a man who has taken in every soul to cross the boundaries of the Seven Devils Ranch and served them a portion of his generous and unending hospitality. I give you…Uncle Nick."

Thunderous applause broke out. The company raised their glasses to the older man who sternly told them they should eat before everything ruined.

After giving Shelby another sip from his glass, Beau placed his lips at the same spot and finished off the punch. The delicate color in her face deepened, acknowledging that she'd noted his action, as he'd intended.

An electric current zinged through him. As a doctor, he knew his eyes would have dilated somewhat, his pulse would be faster and blood would be speeding to the nether regions of his body in response to the wild hunger that gnawed at his control. Had they been alone he would have kissed her.

Had they been alone, would kisses have been enough?

Not for long, he admitted. He let his gaze linger on her mouth. When he realized he was making her uncomfortable, he forced his attention to the front of the tent where guests were lining up for the banquet.

"Here, let's grab a table." He pulled out a chair and seated Shelby, brought over the infant's stroller and took a chair for himself. "I'll fix us plates when the line thins out," he promised.

"Never mind, cuz," Trevor said, bringing over two plates. "I got it covered."

"Thanks, Trev, for thinking of us," Beau drawled. He took the two plates from his cousin and put them on the table for Shelby and himself.

"Hey!" Trevor gave him a glare, then shrugged. "Okay, okay, I'll get another for myself."

"And find another table," Beau called after him. "I'll get drinks. What would you like?" he asked Shelby.

"Iced tea, please."

When he returned, Roni and Seth had joined the group. Janis had reclaimed her son, put him in the stroller and wheeled him away. Beau sat next to Shelby.

"This has been a busy weekend," Roni declared. "Did anyone know about Janis and Keith?"

"It was a surprise to me," Seth said.

"Same here." Beau grinned. "I'll bet it wasn't to Uncle Nick."

Roni looked thoughtful. "You may be right. Last week he took a bunch of stuff from the garden over to their place. He probably gave them one of his famous lectures on duty, marriage and child-rearing."

Shelby looked up. "Speaking of duty, I think I was supposed to do something at the punch bowl."

"No need," Roni told her. "Mrs. Harvey and Uncle Nick are duking it out over who's in charge. She's got the cake knife and he's got the punch ladle."

Beau laid a dollar on the table. "My money's on Uncle Nick."

"I don't know," Seth drawled. "Women are a pretty mean bunch to cross."

Roni smacked him on the arm. "Sexist."

Beau put his dollar up since no one accepted his bet. He was aware of Shelby, looking like an enchanted swan, her hair swept up on her head in an old-fashioned style. He thought of removing the pins one by one until it tumbled around them.

Although she smiled, she mostly listened rather

than took part in the conversation. Occasionally her gaze roamed around the yard. Following her line of vision, he found she often observed the two newly married couples. No, not the adults, it was the baby that intrigued her.

Interesting.

In the two weeks he'd worked with Shelby, he'd found her efficient and highly competent. She was friendly, but not effusive. Brisk, but never rushed. Sympathetic without being sentimental. She was also introspective, but not to the point of distraction.

Not usually, he amended, recalling the day they'd examined the kindergarten kids. Low blood sugar, as he'd thought then? Or, noting her glance at Janis as she fed the baby, something more?

As Shelby raised the tea glass to her lips, he observed the tremor in her hand. When her eyes met his, he saw the awareness flash through the mysterious depths. So, was the nervousness because of him? Did he affect her as much as she did him? Or was he being an egotistical maniac?

When her arm accidentally brushed his, she put more distance between them than he liked. Her glance made it clear she wanted the space.

Okay, so he was an egotistical maniac.

She caught his smile as he laughed at himself. She fascinated him, this lovely woman who had left an excellent position for a part-time job in the middle of nowhere. He wanted to learn her secrets. All of them.

* * *

''Come on, we're touring the newlyweds' house,'' someone called to the group that was left at the reception.

Shelby noticed that most people had left, either to go to their own ranches and attend to chores or to head back to town as twilight changed the landscape to the softer shades of the coming night.

Fatigue dogged her footsteps as she followed the dozen remaining guests on a short path through the woods. She wished she could ask Beau to take her home, but she didn't feel it was right to take him away from his family. In the future, she would provide her own transportation.

At the end of the path, they found a modern home tucked into a clearing among the evergreen trees. Several people murmured in surprise. It was lovely.

The house had four bedrooms, large enough for a family with two, three, even four children. The layout was open and inviting, with a cozy ambience that welcomed and urged one to linger in the pleasant surroundings.

The home reminded her of the happy plans she'd once made, sure that all was right in her world. Such confidence. Where had it come from?

Heaviness settled over her, as if weights had been strapped on each shoulder. Holding the baby—Keith Junior, called K.J.—had been the hardest thing. However, she didn't think anyone noticed. Being a nurse, she'd had to learn to maintain distance from her own emotions.

Beau took her arm as they descended the steps after the tour of the new house. "Ready to go home?"

She nodded and gratefully followed him down the path. At the main ranch house, she thanked his uncle for a lovely day, said her farewells to the rest of the Dalton clan, then went with Beau to his truck rather than the station wagon they had arrived in.

"We'll leave the royal chariot in case Uncle Nick has other VIP guests," he said, giving her a smile. He removed his coat and tie, tossed them behind the seat, then started off. His sister waved goodbye.

Shelby was aware of his thoughtful glance several times as they returned to the small town and the cottage by the lake. She hadn't the energy to think up small talk.

"How about some coffee?" he asked when they arrived.

She hesitated, then nodded. He followed her inside. Once the coffee was made, they sat on the porch and watched the shadows deepen over the lake.

Beau watched as a fisherman pulled a four-inch trout from the water. Releasing the small fry, he packed up his gear and headed for the recreation vehicle resort on the other side of the narrow lake. Only the soft sound of waves lapping at the shoreline broke the silence after that.

Shelby emitted an audible sigh.

"Tired?" Beau asked lazily.

"Some." She kicked her sandals aside and tucked her feet under her on the wicker chair.

"You've met the whole family now. What did you think of them?"

"Everyone was very nice, very…very welcoming."

"So you were comfortable at the ranch?"

"Yes, of course."

"What bothered you about today?"

The question caught her off guard. "I don't know what you mean."

"I think you do," he said. He swung his gaze from the lake to her. "Was it the baby? Did it bother you when Janis asked you to hold him?"

She realized she hadn't hidden her feelings as well as she thought she had. "Not at all. He was a sweet baby."

"Keep lying. Maybe I'll believe you. More important, maybe you'll believe yourself."

She stood abruptly and paced away from that all-seeing stare he directed at her. All the tensions of the reception rolled into a ball of mixed emotions. When the baby had quieted under her care, then drifted into sleep, it was as if her heart had been ripped open and all the secret anguish of holding her own child had returned.

Hands closed on her upper arms. "Tell me what makes you sad," he murmured. His lips touched her hair gently.

"Everything, sometimes," she admitted. "A beautiful sunset. A birdcall at twilight. The sky reflected in the lake.'' Her voice dropped a register. ''The perfect innocence of a child.''

''You like children. Is that why you became a pediatrics nurse?''

She felt the probing intelligence behind the question. A warning crept through her. She'd given something away today, some chance expression of the heaviness within had escaped, and he'd caught it. His hands tightened slightly.

''Yes.'' She spoke in a barely heard whisper. The weight pressed against her chest. Pressure built behind her eyes. Tears welled, but only in her heart.

''Then why give up a desirable position to come out here for two part-time jobs?''

She pulled the nearly shattered remnant of composure around her. ''Why do you want to know?''

''Curiosity, I guess.'' He tugged gently until she turned to face him. ''I want to know the real you, the one you hide behind a polite facade...and wistful eyes.''

Resisting the urge to look away, she lifted her chin and gave him her coolest smile. ''Wistful eyes? Is that a diagnosis, Doctor?''

''Maybe.'' He calmly waited for an answer.

She realized he was infinitely patient. He'd wait her out, and someday, in a weak moment, she might tell him. The Dalton family knew most of the families in the county. They might even know hers. If she but confessed her mission, he could help her in the search.

But that was a leap of trust she wasn't quite ready

to make. "I grew restless," she told him. "I wanted something different, except I didn't know what it was."

He leaned closer. "Do you know now?"

She looked up at him and shook her head. "It's silly—"

"No," he contradicted. "Nothing that involves the heart is silly. But it can hurt sometimes."

"Were you hurt?"

"No," he said. "But I think you were."

She quickly shook her head. The pressure on her chest increased until she breathed in shallow drafts, each one bringing a jab of pain. Neither spoke for a minute.

"Let's walk," he said. "Change clothes and we'll hike to the dam and back."

Glad of an escape, she went into the bedroom and quickly changed to knit slacks, a tank top with a matching long-sleeved shirt and sneakers. When she returned, he'd unbuttoned his cuffs and rolled up his sleeves.

"Do you want to lock up?" he asked.

She shook her head and pocketed her wallet. They left by the back way and headed down the rock-and-pine straw path toward the dam. Fifteen minutes later, they stood on the bridge that topped the dam and watched a man and a boy fish along the shore where the reservoir narrowed.

"Let's see if any water is going over," Beau suggested.

Crossing the road, they peered into the narrow canyon with steep walls that had once been a rapidly flowing river. Water gushed in a plume from the lower spillway, a ghostly white spray against the charcoal shadows of evening.

The tension seeped from her soul. When she took a deep breath and let it out in near contentment, he took her hand.

"Ready?"

She nodded.

They strolled homeward along the path. People were inside their houses or rental cabins now, reading or catching the news on television or simply chatting. She and Beau had the lake path to themselves.

As they neared the cottage, he spoke. "You didn't eat much at the reception. Would you like to go over to the Crow's Nest for dinner?"

She shook her head. "I have a pizza in the freezer."

"Good. Let's nuke it, then eat out on the porch."

"It's the kind you have to bake."

"Even better. I hope it has double cheese."

She turned on the oven while he disposed of the wrappings on the pizza. She added more cheese before sliding it onto an oven shelf and setting the timer. Turning around, she found his eyes on her, the hunger open and ravenous.

"I don't have beer. Would you like a glass of wine?"

"Yes."

The tension slammed into her as if she'd thrown on the brakes too fast and caused a rear-end collision. She poured wine into two glasses, handed one to him and fled to the porch, which was less intimate than the tiny house.

At least she'd thought it would be. But the darkness enclosed the screened room in misty magic while the last light glowed briefly behind the peaks and sent ripples of pewter over the lake as the breeze picked up.

"The gloaming," she said, choosing the rocker. "That's what my grandmother called this time of day."

"I like that. It sounds right…soft…mysterious… beckoning."

His voice was like a caress, reminding her of how his hands had felt as he'd stroked her nape, then lifted her hair to kiss her there.

"Shelby," he murmured. "Come sit by me."

He sat on the glider and laid one arm across the back, an invitation that she couldn't ignore.

"I think…"

His smile flashed, and a sparkle gleamed from his eyes. "Try not to," he encouraged.

She could have resisted mockery, but not the sweetly sensitive humor, as if he laughed at both of them and the golden arcs of attraction that bound them as surely as hemp-hewn ropes. She sighed and looked away without moving.

He did laugh now, as if he knew her thoughts exactly.

They sipped the wine in silence until the timer went off. She dashed to the kitchen as if answering a fire bell. When she returned with plates and the food, leaving the kitchen light on so they could see to eat, she was calm again. Well, almost calm.

It struck her as ominous—to come all this way in search of her birth parents and to find this consuming passion instead. She was wise enough to know this portended no good for her heart…and foolish enough not to care, not at this moment.

''Eat,'' he ordered softly.

She did, but his eyes told her this was only a foretaste of the feast that would come later. Maybe not tonight, but sometime…some night…some magical moment…

From across the lake came the enchanting sound of music, hushed and plangent. The Saturday night entertainment at the restaurant had begun.

Beau stood. Hooking an arm around the kitchen door frame, he flicked off the light. ''Dance?'' He held out his hand, his eyes daring her to accept.

Should she? Or should she run as fast and as far as she could?

Chapter Seven

Shelby rose as if pulled by a puppet master. Beau held her formally, three inches of space between them. They began to dance a slow two-step to the haunting melody. After a minute, he pulled her closer, gently, carefully, testing her reaction each inch of the way.

When they were touching and his cheek rested against her temple, he sighed as if content.

"You're a good dancer," she murmured.

"Uncle Nick got a video and tried to make us guys learn ballroom dancing. Since we only had each other for partners and Roni refused to dance with any of us, he didn't have much success."

"So how did you learn?"

"I sneaked and watched the video several times, then practiced on my own when no one was around."

She enjoyed his story. "Your family seems to have had a lot of fun and camaraderie." It wasn't until she'd spoken that she realized how wistful she sounded.

He shrugged and urged her head to his shoulder. "We were like any other family. There were good moments and there were bad ones."

"Did the first outweigh the second?"

"Yeah. Overall, it did. What about you?"

"The same, I think. My father has three older sisters. When we read Shakespeare in school, I often thought of them as the three witches."

"Bubble, bubble, toil and trouble?"

"Yes. Without their direct supervision, they thought the world was going to hell in a handbasket, my dad used to say. They were bossy, but I enjoyed their visits. What kid wouldn't? I was the center of attention. They taught me to embroider and crochet and knit."

"Did you have any siblings?"

"No. I was a…an only child." She'd started to say "adopted," but caught herself. She wasn't ready to disclose that much about herself. It might lead to questions about her motives for being in Lost Valley, and she still had the copper bracelet to check out as well as the medical records.

"Were you lonely?"

"Actually, no."

"Did the sisters have children?"

"No. One was widowed shortly after she married, one was divorced, the youngest never wed. My mother has a younger brother. He and his wife have two daughters. I loved it when they visited, but my cousins fought a lot. That made me glad I didn't have to share my room and toys with a sister and that they lived in Oklahoma so they didn't visit too often."

He laughed, a rich sound that reached right down into her soul. When the slow music ended and a faster beat started, he returned to the glider. Her hand was still in his when he sat. He tugged slightly, inviting her to join him but not insisting.

Taking the place beside him, she let her gaze roam over the scenery. Night had truly fallen and the sky was awash with stars, more than she'd ever seen.

"There're more stars here than at home," she said.

He idly lifted a lock of her hair and brought it to his lips. "It's the lack of artificial light. The sky is darker, so the stars show up better."

From the corner of her eye, she could see the way he brushed the curl against his mouth, as if intrigued by it.

"Your hair is like a cool fire, one that glows but doesn't get hot enough to burn," he said. "It smells of balsam and spices."

The heaviness within her changed, becoming not exactly lighter, but more bearable. The air between them became charged with currents that whispered of need and yearning and hopes long forgotten. She wanted to curl up against him and absorb his essence...

Fear interwove with the hunger. She was silent for a minute, then said, "It's getting late."

"We can sleep in tomorrow."

The words and their implication sent shock waves rolling through her while she sat as if cast in a deep spell. She wasn't even sure she was breathing.

"Can't we?" he asked. He slipped a hand into her hair and turned her face to his. "I want to sleep in. With you."

"We can't."

"Why?"

"It might... It could lead to...complications," she finished, and irrationally hoped he would sweep her arguments right away.

His lips were very near hers. He looked into her eyes. "Tell me now if you want me to leave," he advised in a low, husky voice. "If I kiss you, it'll be too late."

Her heart drummed in her ears, drowning out all other sounds, including any protests her conscience might make.

"Shall I leave?"

She opened her mouth, but didn't speak.

"Or stay?" He bent his head closer to hers. "Leave? Or stay? It's up to you."

"I think you should..." The command to go wouldn't leave her lips "...stay."

Her thoughts scattered like playful mice in a cornfield as his mouth crashed down on hers, intent and demanding and so very, very necessary. How, she wondered, astonished, had she lived so long without this?

The kiss was hot and wild and infinitely sweet. It made her ache in a secret place only vaguely recalled from long ago, from that time when she'd been young and filled with all the confidence of youth.

When she slipped her fingers into his midnight dark hair, he made a little sound deep in his throat, a growl of pleasure that set off an answering purr in her.

"Yes," she said as he pressed her against the glider arm and laid a line of kisses along her throat to the edge of the tank top. "Oh, yes."

"Every morning, when you arrive at the office, I want to do this—to taste each part and compare it to the dreams I have of you, of us, together like this."

"I could see it in your eyes. It got so I didn't dare look at you. It was too dangerous."

He laughed at her confession. "You did a darned good job of disguising that fact. I thought it was all one-sided on my part."

"It wasn't," she answered, unable to lie.

Kiss followed kiss. Like the stars, there were too many to be counted. Slowly the barriers came down, melted beyond repair by his gentle caresses. His skillful fingers swept over her in gentle forays.

Cherished, she thought at one point. She now knew the meaning of the word.

Clothing was unfastened, pushed aside. Hands

reached eagerly beneath the bunched material to find warm, living flesh. Arms and thighs locked in a passionate embrace as they tried to touch everywhere.

But there was only so much they could do, half lying, half sitting in a tangle on the short glider. When she shifted to ease the crook in her neck, he pushed upright. The glider jerked and swayed. They slid precariously near the edge.

"Let's go in," he murmured with an undercurrent of laughter. "I'm sure we can find a more comfortable place."

Shelby's heart pounded loudly as she led the way inside the cottage. Beau closed and locked the kitchen door behind them while she checked the front door. They met at the entry to the bedroom and halted, their eyes locked.

Even in the near dark, she could see the question in his eyes and knew she could still change her mind. Against all good sense, she knew she wasn't going to. Stepping close, she put her arms around him and rested her head against his chest. His heartbeat was strong and steady, as loud as hers.

"Come," she said, and led the way.

He helped her undress, his hands sure at the task. When she shivered as the chill air from the mountains flowed around them, he urged her into bed and quickly tossed his own clothing on a chair with hers. He quickly rolled a condom in place before sliding in under the sheet.

When he embraced her…when his lean, hard body

pressed ardently against hers, she realized that not even in her younger, most idealistic days had she felt this intensity of passion. It burned as clear and pure as the fire upon some ancient altar.

Emotion leaped brightly within, a hint of warning in its fiery turbulence.

Before she had time to consider this development, she was consumed by the hunger as his hands roamed all over her.

She touched him, too, in the same way he did her. She liked his little gasp of passion and the deep groan her caresses elicited.

When his lips followed the same meandering path of his hands as he explored her body in fine detail, she found she couldn't contain the panting cries that rose from her throat. When she couldn't bear it another second, he came to her, merging them into one sweet whole.

"Like fire," he whispered into her hair, "inside and out, all around us."

"Yes." She knew exactly what he meant. "I want... I've never..."

He brushed the tendrils of tangled curls off her forehead and looked into her eyes. "It's the same for me. Nothing has ever been this strong, this urgent."

For another moment she held his gaze, then she had to close her eyes as waves of desire rose and crashed against her self-control. He moved gently against her, then faster as she urged him closer.

Beau caught her cry of ecstasy with a kiss. The taut

leash he'd kept on his hunger slipped away and he thrust deeply, a low groan torn from him as he found his own satisfaction. He continued moving until he felt her relax completely in his arms.

When they could breathe easily once more, he turned so that they lay side by side. "Of all the best kisses in the whole world, that was number one," he said.

In the silvery play of moonlight through the open window, he saw her smile once, then she snuggled close and sighed as if she'd just completed a long journey.

Maybe both of them had. He just didn't know from where...or to what final destination.

Shelby woke to the rumble of thunder. Through the window, she could see black thunderclouds over the peaks. An arm lay over her middle, holding her in a warm embrace.

Hardly daring to breathe, she slipped out of bed and into the bathroom. There, she quickly adjusted the shower and stepped inside, her mind blanketed with contentment.

She would have to think about last night sometime, but not now. It was too peaceful to just drift—

"May I join you?" a deep voice asked.

A momentary shyness washed over her and she could only nod. His smile was so warm it helped put her at ease.

He squirted a generous dollop of bath gel into his

palm, then leisurely worked up a lather and massaged it over her shoulders and down her spine. Slowly he wended his way over her body, pressing his chest to her back as he slid soapy hands around her waist, over her abdomen and up to her breasts. Her nipples contracted so hard, she gasped.

He swept her wet hair aside and kissed her neck, then his hands became more intimate upon her.

"My legs are going weak," she warned as tremors ran over her.

"Lean into me," he said in a deepened voice.

They spent long, wonderful moments in the shower. Finally he turned the water off and, not letting her help, dried them both. They returned to the bedroom just as a long boom of thunder rolled across the valley.

"Which is greater," he asked, "the storm within or the one without?"

"It's a toss-up," she declared.

The morning was as passionate as the night. When they at last rested, content in each other's arms, they watched the storm linger over the mountains. Streaks of gray indicated rain on the highest peaks, but none fell in the valley.

He pushed the sheet aside after a while and idly ran his hand over her breasts and down to her waist. He propped himself up on his other arm, a slight smile curving his lips as he gazed at her body.

She realized she felt beautiful and desirable for the first time in a long time. And that she felt no regrets.

Perhaps they would come, but not yet. Today she simply wanted to bask in the passionate afterglow.

From the kitchen came the beep of the coffeemaker. He glanced at her in question.

"The coffee is ready. It's on a timer so I can prepare it the night before. It wakes me up in the mornings. Usually," she added.

He smiled. "I'm hungry. How about you?"

"Yes." She shifted and he let her go.

He pulled on his clothing while she rummaged through a basket of clean clothes. Upon finding her favorite sweats, she quickly dressed and donned thick socks. When she glanced at him once more, she found he was following her every move.

It made her a little self-conscious. His gaze was thoughtful, but she couldn't read what he was thinking.

"Pancakes? Eggs? An omelet?" she asked, heading for the kitchen.

"Pancakes would be great. Uncle Nick used to make them every Sunday morning when we were kids. I'm too lazy to bother, but that's still my favorite breakfast."

She gave him a mug of coffee, then prepared pancakes with fresh mountain blueberries and a side order of ham.

By the time they finished the meal, the storm had passed and the sun was shining. When the Sunday paper arrived, she brought it in, poured fresh cups of coffee and gave him the front section while she read the comics.

Catching his gaze, which had lingered on her at odd moments since he'd awakened, she realized something was on his mind and asked, "What is it?"

His smile was breathtaking, bone-jarring, soul-stirring. All of the above. He shook his head slightly, his nearly black hair sweeping over his forehead in attractive disarray.

"You," Beau murmured. "Just you."

The hum of sexual contentment ran through his body, but even that wasn't enough to cancel the questions this intriguing woman raised in him. He considered asking them, but instinctively knew this wasn't the time.

Or maybe he was a coward. He didn't want to shatter the moment or the sweet memories of the night.

"What do you think of the house?" he asked instead.

"I love it," she admitted. "Did you buy it for a rental property, or to add to the lodge? It would make a neat home for the resort manager, private but close by."

"Actually I bought it for me. I thought it would make a great location for a home for a busy family doctor with a local practice."

Emotion ran through her eyes, but was gone before he could read it. Longing? Envy? That inexplicable sadness he sometimes detected in her?

"Does that idea bother you?" he asked.

She shook her head. "Of course not. You're right. This would be an ideal place for a...for a family."

He took note of the hesitation in mentioning a family. "Speaking of family, I must confess I heard you speaking on the phone to yours. I came over after working next door the other night. Before I could knock, I heard your voice and thought you already had company. I was jealous."

His confession surprised her and distracted her, as he'd planned.

"Then I realized, since I only heard you, that you must be on the phone. When you referred to your father, I knew you were talking to your family and crept away so you wouldn't catch me eavesdropping. Are your parents originally from the South?"

"Yes. Other than a stint in the army and at college, my dad has lived in the same town all his life."

"You said your mother was from Kentucky?"

"Yes. She and my father met on spring break in Daytona Beach, Florida. They married as soon as he graduated. My grandparents were horrified at the thought of the fast woman who had snared their son."

Her laughter was natural and unforced as she recounted the story. Beau smiled, too. "But the marriage has lasted."

"Yes. They worked together and started a fast-food franchise out on the highway. It was a success, and they own several now. Mom is the CEO because she's better with people. Dad is the treasurer because he'd rather deal with numbers and inventory."

"Sounds like a working team."

She nodded, her smile growing nostalgic.

"Do you miss your home?" he asked.

"Some," she admitted, then added, "but I love it here, too. The mountains offer the same sense of eternity that the ocean does. It reminds me that life goes on…"

That odd sadness flickered through her eyes and was gone. Beau tried to asses its cause and concluded it was more than missing her folks. Was it involved with the quest she was on, the one that could prove dangerous?

He suppressed the impatient questions that rose to his tongue. Grilling her wasn't going to get him answers. She would have to trust him, and her trust would come slowly, he sensed.

Recalling his own childhood fears that Uncle Nick was going to go away and never return—the way his parents and Aunt Millie and Tink had—he backed off from demanding she share all her secrets with him.

"So your parents fell in love at first sight," he said lightly. "What about you? Any old boyfriends languishing on the sandy beaches back home?"

Had he not been watching he might have missed the quick tightening of her hand on the coffee cup. "None," she said softly, her gaze on the mountain scene outside the window.

The word was definitive, and he knew she wasn't lying. However, she wasn't telling everything, either.

She had stretch marks, thin lines on her breasts that

most people wouldn't notice. The marks were usually accounted for by one of two things: an advanced state of pregnancy or a substantial weight loss.

Since nothing indicated she'd ever been heavy, he reached the logical conclusion. She'd once had a child.

Shelby was glad the next day was Monday. Work forced her back on an even keel with Beau, and she was glad to get out of the cottage. Now that she knew his plans for the charming site, she kept thinking of ways to enlarge it into a family home. There would have to be a safety fence for the children because of the lake—

Gritting her teeth, she forced the intrusive ideas aside as she weighed a baby for its one-year checkup. "Twenty pounds," she told the mother, lifting the infant from the scale.

The baby slipped a hand inside Shelby's white jacket and clasped the tank top strap. A sharp painful contraction ran through her breasts. As she returned the child to its mother, she glanced up and met Beau's thoughtful gaze.

Heat raced over her. Keeping distance between them after the intimacy of the weekend was as difficult as she'd thought it would be. She had carefully timed her arrival that morning for a couple of minutes before eight so they wouldn't be alone. He'd realized that immediately.

Handing over the chart, she left the doctor with the

mother and patient. She finished up her duties, told Bertie she was off, and quickly left the clinic. After eating lunch at the cottage, she reported in for the first day of the new school year. She was busy for the rest of the afternoon.

At four she left the school grounds and, afraid to be alone at the cottage, jogged for an hour, then finished with a walk along the lake. The evening was quiet as families settled in for the dinner hour. Even the construction around the lake, which went on from dawn until dark most days, was silent. Twilight spread deep shadows across the landscape before she returned home.

"Oh," she said, startled by the person on her porch.

"Surprised?" Beau asked, rising from the glider and holding the screen door open for her.

She nodded, experiencing an almost painful shyness as they faced each other at the scene of the crime, so to speak. "I wasn't expecting you."

"I thought we needed to talk."

He thrust his hands into the pockets of his jeans. The work shirt was unbuttoned over a tank top. He looked ready for another eight hours of work, tireless and capable and handsome as only a supremely fit male specimen could be.

"What about?" she asked, her mind going blank. She blotted her face with the end of her T-shirt, knowing she must look totally frazzled.

His snort of laughter was ironic rather than amused.

"Come talk to me while I work. I agreed to do the caulking while Trevor's on the rodeo circuit. He's a stickler for sealing every crack and crevice, says that costs less in the long run for heating and cooling."

"I'm sure that's true. Uh, I need to shower and change, then eat."

"Let's order something," he suggested.

She thought of the intimacy of sharing a meal and shook her head. "I should... I have things to do."

He came close. His scent was fresh, as if he'd showered before coming over. "The weekend was one of the best I've ever experienced."

"That was unwise."

"I'm not sorry," he said softly. "Are you?"

She hesitated, then nodded. "It's a complication I don't want."

"What do you want?"

Looking into his eyes, she was seized with a desire to tell him everything and to enlist his help in her quest. She shook her head slightly, negating the impulsive thought. Pulling up a smile, she said, "A chance to find myself, I think. That's why I wanted to get away from my home and parents and those who think they know best for me."

"Were there also painful memories?"

She nodded, realizing he sensed something of the conflict in her and perhaps something of her goals. She'd let him come too close. "I need some time. Alone," she added. "I have things I need to think about."

He looked as if he would ask more questions, but finally he released a heavy breath and nodded. "I'll give you space if that's what you want, but if you need someone to talk to, give me a yell."

She nodded. He bent toward her and she raised her face for his light kiss without thinking. When he left, she watched him cross the lawn to the lodge, his stride long and easy, as if the world belonged to him.

For a moment she wanted to rush after him, to tell him she'd changed her mind and wanted him to stay with her. She sighed and forced her feet toward the bathroom and a cool-down period in the shower.

A minute later she stepped into the shower and let the water cascade over her. With her eyes closed, she shivered as memories—fresh ones that had nothing to do with the days of her youth—washed over her.

However she couldn't plan a future without knowing the past. That's why she was here and what she had to remember instead of sexy blue eyes and hands that knew just how to touch and tease and caress. With Beau to distract her, she was in danger of losing sight of her goal.

Chapter Eight

The clinic was closed on Wednesday so Shelby used the morning for her search. Unwrapping the copper bracelet, she slipped it into a plastic bag and put it in her purse, then headed out on the highway toward the county seat.

A couple of telephone calls had disclosed that the original store where the bracelet was sold had gone out of business years ago, the mom-and-pop owners deceased. However, there was another place that sold Native American jewelry and they might know the family who'd made the bracelet. So, that was where she was going.

Thirty minutes later she pulled into the parking lot of the Trading Post, a store catering to tourists who wanted a souvenir of their vacation in the area. The inside was eerily empty of either tourists or employees. She walked along the aisles, gazing intently at the goods on display.

"Be with you in a moment," a masculine voice called from the back.

"Thanks," she answered, forcing a casualness to her voice that she was far from feeling.

Stopping in front of a rack of copper earrings, she looked them over. Nothing resembled the design of her bracelet.

Then her gaze was drawn downward and she gasped, her hand going to her chest. Her heart pounded so loud, she could hear it. Inside the case were dozens of items fashioned in copper, silver and gold. Carved stones decorated some of the most expensive jewelry.

They were similar to the bracelet in her purse, each crafted of metal strands, some finer than silk threads, woven around and over each other into intricate love knots and floral or geometric designs. The prices were shocking.

"Lovely, aren't they? Each is handmade and one of a kind. The wire wrap is exquisite, requiring many hours."

She glanced up at the man who appeared behind the counter. He was tall and dark, his black hair tied with a rawhide thong at his nape, his eyes blue-gray with brown flecks. "Are they made locally?"

She'd already composed a list of questions and waited anxiously for his answer to her first one.

"Yes." His smile flashed brilliantly against his deeply tanned face. "My cousins, in fact. I'm Trek Lanigan, owner of this fine establishment."

The last name wasn't the same as the mom-and-pop store owners she'd been looking for. Disappointment hit her, but she smiled politely. "I'm Shelby Wheeling."

"Ah, the new school nurse down at Lost Valley. My nephew started kindergarten this year. He's already fallen hard for you," he explained at her start of surprise.

"Your cousins, are they Native American?"

"Nee-Me-Poo."

She'd read enough about the area to know the name meant "the real people" and was how the Nez Perce referred to themselves. Making a decision, she removed the plastic bag from her purse and slipped the bracelet out.

"Can you tell me if this was made around here?"

The man took the bracelet, studied it, then excused himself. When he headed for a door marked Office, she followed at his heels. There he took a magnifying glass and peered at the underside of the fastener.

"This isn't new," he said.

"It belonged to my mother."

"Did she tell you anything about it?"

Shelby shook her head.

"See these initials?" He handed her the magnifying glass and pointed to the catch. "This bracelet was made by my great-uncle. Do you have an appraisal on it?"

"No. I never thought about it."

"His work is considered museum quality. I'll give you five thousand, no questions asked." He smiled ruefully. "However, you could probably get more at auction."

"I don't want to sell the bracelet. I just want to know something about it. It's…it's all I have of her."

"I'm sorry," he said, obviously assuming her mother was dead. He told her about his uncle's work and explained what each symbol meant.

Shelby listened patiently, then asked about meeting the artisan. The man shook his head. "My uncle died more than ten years ago."

Her spirits dropped. "I was hoping to find my mother's people. I think she was from this area."

"What was her name?"

Shelby considered, then admitted the truth. "Silvers. Sandra Silvers."

No light of recognition dawned in his eyes. "Sorry. The name doesn't ring a bell."

"I wondered—"

The door opened and a family came into the shop. The mother and two teenage girls went at once to the jewelry displays while the man and a boy went to a wall display of bows and arrows.

Trek motioned to a coffeemaker. "Help yourself. I'll be back in a minute."

However the moments stretched to a half hour, then more, as other motorists stopped. Shelby went to the counter. "If you think of anything, let me know," she requested, replacing the bracelet in her purse.

"I will. I'll check with my great-aunt. She might have a suggestion on where you should look."

Shelby didn't pin her hopes on such a flimsy possibility, but she nodded, thanked him sincerely and drove back to Lost Valley. At the grocery, she encountered Amelia from the B and B.

"Come over if you have time," her former landlady invited. "Miss Pickford will be there."

Shelby took her groceries home, then went to the B and B. Amelia had a table for three set with sandwiches and fruit. "It's a tad early, but I thought we could have lunch. I know you have to be at school by twelve."

"Everything looks delicious. Can I help?"

Amelia shook her head. "It's ready. And here's Miss Pickford, right on time."

The older lady entered the common room and joined them at the table. She reported on the progress of the Historical Society. "We have two people researching land titles at the county seat, starting from the oldest records. They're also checking the old mining claims. How are you doing with the medical records?"

Shelby told them she'd gone through the most recent years. Beau had insisted on paying her for sorting through current patients, briefly recording any pertinent info into their folders, then destroying the old records.

"I have a list of names with births and deaths," she told the other two, and fished the notebook from her purse.

The plastic bag containing the bracelet fell to the floor. Amelia picked it up before she could.

"You must have been shopping at The Trading Post," the B and B owner said, admiring the bracelet. "This is lovely."

"I was there this morning," Shelby admitted, letting them think she had just purchased the jewelry.

Glancing at Miss Pickford, she noted the woman sitting perfectly still as if cast in stone. Her eyes, the bright blue of a robin's egg, were on the bracelet. A prickle of unease went through Shelby.

"That isn't new," the older woman said, catching Shelby's gaze on her. "I can't imagine Trek selling an heirloom item. He usually buys all he can find."

The older woman held out her hand. Amelia gave her the bag. Miss Pickford removed the bracelet and studied it with a knowledgeable eye. She turned it over and checked the back, then she gave Shelby a long appraisal as if questioning how she came by the piece. Shelby remained silent. At last, Miss Pickford returned it.

Shelby took the bag and replaced it in her purse. "It was a gift," she said as casually as she could, feeling the need to explain her possession of the unique bracelet. "Are any of these names from the first families?'' she asked, opening the notebook to the list she'd made.

The ploy worked to distract the other two women from the bracelet. Shelby wasn't ready to disclose exactly how she got it, and she could see questions stirring in the astute former schoolmarm. As soon as possible she excused herself to get ready for her afternoon stint at the school.

At the cottage, she studied the piece of jewelry, particularly the initials on the back, which were discernible now that she knew they were there. Sadly, she admitted it was useless. There was no way to trace the owner of the bracelet. The plan had been forlorn from the first.

She stored the piece in the velvet roll-up, locked the cottage and walked to the elementary school three blocks from the house. Two cases of chicken pox awaited her.

''Well,'' Beau said philosophically, ''about one percent of vaccinated kids get chicken pox anyway, so maybe we're not in an epidemic.''

Shelby didn't respond. Today was Friday, and more kids were coming down with chicken pox. She was concerned.

Beau grimaced and nodded. ''Okay, so you think we are in an epidemic.''

''Five cases in a week, two of them severe. I don't think those children were immunized even though their records show they were.''

"Probably not," he agreed. "I'm meeting with the county health department at six tonight to discuss antiviral medication for all kids that we don't have medical records on. Would you mind attending?"

"No, of course not. If you think you need me."

At his silence, she glanced his way.

"Oh, yes, I need you," he said with gentle irony.

Heat flashed through her with the speed of summer lightning. He laughed then, a soft chuckle that sent frissons dancing along her scalp and spine.

Need? That was hardly the term to explain the passion between them, but she understood exactly what he meant.

At night she woke from feverish dreams that left her strung out like too tight piano wire. She alternated between anger with herself for being weak and resentment of him for making her that way. An involvement, she sternly reminded her libido, was a no-win situation. Besides, she had no time for it.

"Where is the meeting?" she asked, to put them firmly back on a professional footing.

"At the health department offices. I'll pick you up."

Before she could protest, the phone rang. While he answered, she returned to the medicine cabinet, made sure it was locked, then drove to the elementary school. The principal was waiting for her. They had two new cases of chicken pox.

The meeting that was supposed to start at six actually got under way at six-forty. The mayor was there with two county commissioners. With Beau, the health nurse and department superintendent, that made six, plus her. They discussed the problems of the disease, which had now cropped up in two other schools. Anti-viral medicine was called for.

"Who's going to come up with the money?" the health superintendent asked.

"What about emergency funds?" the mayor asked.

"We don't have any," the superintendent said glumly. He looked at Beau.

Shelby realized the Dalton family must often provide money or solutions to local problems. That didn't seem exactly fair. "Uh, perhaps we could do some bake sales," she suggested. "The Historical Society might have some ideas for a fund-raiser."

"We need the money now," the health nurse reminded her.

Beau held up a finger, stopping the conversation. "How about having an amateur rodeo at the county fair? Zack has a bunch of cutting horses ready for show. The ranch could supply calves for roping and steers for wrestling. We could charge five dollars a head to attend."

The mayor shook his head. "There's the time factor again. The fair isn't until next month."

"I'll check with the drug companies," Beau promised. "Maybe they'll let us have the medication on consignment until we get the money together. The city council would have to agree to foot the bill."

"Since most of the kids live in the county, I think the county is responsible," the mayor said.

The county commissioners didn't agree.

Beau interrupted the developing quarrel. "I can pledge a thousand dollars toward the cost. Maybe other businesses will, too."

Shelby knew it cost a fortune to set up a new office. The clinic had the latest equipment, including a small but efficient operating theater. She wondered if Beau could really afford to donate money as well as all the free service he gave the community.

Not that it was any of her concern.

The mayor said he would match the pledge... somewhat reluctantly, Shelby thought.

After the meeting, Beau drove her home in the old pickup that was polished to a glossy shine.

Parking in her drive, he said, "Let's walk over to the restaurant. I haven't had dinner yet."

"It's nine," she said, frowning at this indication of irregular eating habits.

"Tell me about it."

He took her arm and guided her to the trail around the lake. She knew she should protest, go to the cottage and lock herself inside before she did something foolish.

"I should—"

"Indulge me," he said.

She fell silent. Finally she sighed, giving in to his request and her own desires. She wasn't being foolish as she'd been at eighteen, she assured herself. This time, she knew what she was doing. And she expected nothing.

Beau ate a bowl of soup and a salad while she yielded to temptation and had blackberry cobbler with ice cream.

"That was worth the extra miles I'll have to run," she said upon finishing.

"You're faithful at your exercise. The carpenters say they see you nearly every day, jogging around the lake."

"Well, I jog for twelve minutes. That's the aerobic part, then I walk for the remainder of the hour. That's to burn off the calories. I hope."

He pushed the empty bowl and plate aside. "I was thinking of you and Honey—that's Zack's wife—yesterday."

"She's the dance teacher," Shelby said, remembering meeting the slender, graceful blonde. "She's using the carriage house at Amelia's B and B for a studio."

"Right. I was thinking you two could work up an exercise class that I could refer patients to. I think every patient I saw yesterday was overweight by at least thirty pounds. We need to do something about that. You could do weigh-ins, then check heart rates during the exercise while Honey incorporates exercise in a dance routine."

Shelby was at once taken with the idea and had several suggestions for encouraging people to take part. "If you wrote them a prescription—so many minutes a week, for instance—then they might do it. But what about snow in the winter?''

''What about it?''

''Well, would they come into town for an exercise class in that case?''

''Hmm, that could be a problem. Not many people are eager to get out when the temperature is hovering at zero. I'd rather stay in front of a crackling fire myself.''

His grin was so engaging, Shelby found herself smiling as she envisioned the fire, two easy chairs and a couple sitting quietly, reading a book…or maybe sharing one of the chairs, talking about their day…

Seeing his frankly sexy gaze on her, she knew that he knew where her mind had gone. She also knew that he knew that she knew…

She halted the convoluted thinking before she drove herself insane. His smile widened.

''Are you thinking about us?'' he demanded softly.

She shook her head, vigorously denying the charge. Meeting his eyes, she realized the question had been rhetorical on his part.

He chuckled.

She couldn't help it; she laughed.

''That's better,'' he said. He laid some cash on the table. ''Ready?''

Taking her hand, he escorted her along the lake path, which was barely visible by the pale light of the moon. Last weekend seemed but a dream while the current one loomed urgent and intense in front of them.

"Have you reached a decision?" he asked when they arrived at the cottage door.

"What decision?" she asked, startled by the question.

"You've argued with yourself all the way here. Are you going to invite me in?"

"No. I shouldn't," she amended, then realized she was waffling when she'd meant to stand firm.

"Why not?" He looped a flyaway strand of hair behind her ear, his touch as gentle as she remembered.

"An affair is out of the question," she stated primly. "We're professionals, working in the same office."

He didn't argue.

"It isn't wise to get involved."

"True."

She frowned at the agreement. "Things could get too complicated."

He was silent for a few seconds. "I think they already are complicated."

His tone brought her up short. "What do you mean?" she asked, trying to read his expression in the dim light.

"Trek Lanigan out at the Trading Post said you had a bracelet made by his great-uncle and you were asking about it the other day."

The gift shop was thirty miles from here. Shelby

hadn't thought about her search becoming known in town.

"He said it was a gift from your mother."

"Yes, it was."

She waited for him to probe further. Taking a step back, she resisted an urge to rush inside and lock the door. She wasn't ready for her life story to be general knowledge in the town. Not yet.

"When he told me about the bracelet, I wanted to know more." Beau stepped close. "I want to understand the mystery that surrounds you."

Relief left her weak-kneed. Apparently the store owner hadn't shared the rest of her confidences. "There is no mystery."

"I think there is."

If he'd been accusing or angry, she could have handled him better, but he was none of those. Instead, his tone was gentle, as if he sought understanding.

The urge to confess all rushed over her. Perhaps it would be better to bring her quest into the open. Maybe someone would contact her if they knew about it. But maybe not. Her birth mother had kept the secret for almost thirty years. Without some understanding of the circumstances, Shelby couldn't bring herself to break that silence.

"You're wrong," she told her inquisitor.

"All right," he said. "There's something else I've wondered about."

Before she could ask what it was, he moved closer, then his lips were near hers, then they were touching.

A sharp pain jangled along her nerves. She'd wanted this, she admitted. All week, in the office and out, she'd thought about his kisses. The memory of his touch had haunted her every moment of every day.

She made no protest when he gathered her into his arms, melding them into one. The kiss stretched into a moment, then another. Eternity beckoned. She wanted...she wanted...so many things.

A cry of despair rose to her lips and she pulled away, trembling with the need to know him completely, to share all that she was with him. "Don't," she whispered.

He dropped his hands to his sides, his breath coming fast. "What are you afraid of?"

"You." She tried to laugh but the attempt sounded feeble even to her.

"I'm the one who should be afraid." He brushed his thumb over her lips. "You've got me in your snare. What are your intentions?"

He dropped his hand. Her lips felt forlorn, cool without his warming touch.

"I never meant for this to happen. I came here to—" She stopped before revealing too much. "I wanted to see more of the world, to find something different."

And she had. In his arms, she'd found more than she'd ever imagined.

"Or were you running from something?" he asked.

"No, I wasn't."

He heaved a deep breath. "I believe you. Maybe

you were running *to* something. Us,'' he added as a suggestion, the wry humor back in his voice.

The tension suddenly eased. She realized he was backing off, giving her space and letting her keep her secrets. For now. She knew the reprieve wouldn't last forever.

''Good night, sweet temptress,'' he murmured, then left after he saw her safely inside the cottage, the door locked securely between them.

She went to the living room and leaned against the window frame, watching until the lights of the old pickup faded from sight. She touched her lips carefully, as if he'd left a mark there and she didn't want to disturb it.

Standing in the dark, she admitted a fact she'd known all week. She was very close to falling in love with the handsome doctor. Very, very close.

She stood still, as if clinging to the edge of the abyss. If she couldn't risk having children, would it matter to him?

An image of his close-knit family came to her. That in itself was answer enough.

Beau helped himself to two more pancakes and another slice of bacon before laying the fork aside. He settled back in the chair with his coffee cup and took a chug of the strong brew. ''Ah, heaven,'' he declared.

On Sunday morning he'd headed to the ranch at

first light and his favorite breakfast with his favorite relative.

His uncle peered at him, then laid the newspaper aside. "Why didn't you bring that new nurse out?" he demanded. "She would probably enjoy getting away from town and the traffic and all."

Beau didn't comment on the older man's idea of heavy traffic. It was all relative. In Boise, weekends were less hectic than weekdays. In Lost Valley, the local ranchers and their wives came to town for supplies on Saturdays or for church on Sundays and stayed for lunch either day.

"Zack bought a sweet mare the other day," Uncle Nick continued. "You could teach her to ride—uh, the nurse, not the mare."

"Shelby," Beau said. "Shelby Wheeling."

"I know her name." Uncle Nick gave him an exasperated glare. "She was a real help at the wedding, a gal who isn't afraid to pitch in and work. A nurse would make a good mother," he added guilelessly.

A picture of Shelby holding the baby came to Beau. The look in her eyes...haunted, that was the word.

He broke into his favorite relative's not-too-subtle hints about marrying and settling down. "I don't think she's here looking for a husband."

"You can convince her otherwise. My grandmother always said a Dalton could talk a dog out of his tail."

Beau smiled, but went on with his train of thought. "I wondered, when I saw her résumé, why someone with her skills would come to a small town. I think I found out yesterday.''

''Well?'' Uncle Nick said after a brief silence.

''I'm pretty sure she's looking for her birth parents. Trek Lanigan said she came to The Trading Post and wanted to know about a bracelet, a gift from her mother, she said. He thought the mother was dead, but that isn't the case. Unless Shelby was adopted.''

That made his uncle sit up and take notice.

''She isn't Tink,'' Beau said gently. ''There's no scar.''

''They fade with time. Maybe…''

Beau shook his head.

''She has those blue eyes,'' Uncle Nick said.

Beau winced at the wistful tone. Uncle Nick's three-year-old daughter had been kidnapped from the scene of an accident in which her mother had died twenty-two years ago.

Marital joy had come late in his uncle's life and the tragedy had nearly broken the stalwart rancher, but with six orphans to raise, he'd shouldered the burden and never complained. However, he did try to marry off his niece and nephews at every likely opportunity.

''Besides, if the birth date in her records is correct,'' Beau said, ''she's older than Tink would be now by almost four years.''

Uncle Nick gave up on his fantasy. ''So she's looking for her family.'' He nodded wisely. ''A person needs to know these things, their roots and all.''

"I suppose." Beau watched the faint swirl of steam rising from his cup. "There's something else."

His uncle waited silently.

"She's had a child."

The blue eyes so like his own flicked to him, worry in their depths. Beau grimaced at the questions in his uncle's eyes.

"At least I think so," he added truthfully. "She hasn't confided in me, but there are indications of an advanced pregnancy at one time."

"You've slept with her," Uncle Nick at once deduced.

The heat rose to Beau's ears. He nodded.

Uncle Nick started to speak.

"We haven't discussed marriage," Beau said quickly to forestall the next logical conclusion from the old man.

Uncle Nick leveled a stern gaze on him. "A man ought to take responsibility for his impulses."

Beau mentally flinched. To his uncle, everything was black and white. He wished life was that simple.

"I've asked about her reasons for being here, but she clams up at any mention of her past. I don't think she trusts me."

"Maybe she was hurt real bad one time. That makes a person cautious-like. You've been working together almost a month. She's bound to see how steady and honorable you are."

Beau knew his uncle was making assumptions

about his feelings for Shelby and hers for him. He sighed, troubled for reasons he couldn't quite name.

There was the attraction between them, yes. She was the most exciting woman he'd ever met. They worked together as a team with no friction. He liked being with her...okay, so he made excuses to see her even on days she wasn't scheduled to be at the office.

On the negative side was the mystery surrounding her past and her reason for giving up a good position to be a school nurse in a small town so far from her home. And the fact that she hadn't confided in him even after the intimacy they'd shared. Plus, she'd told Trek Lanigan something of her past, but it didn't match the story she'd told him.

Well, to be fair, she'd needed information from Trek if she was trying to trace her parents.

"I'm glad to see you're over Julie," Uncle Nick said, looking solemn but pleased. "You and Trevor had a hard time of it when she and Travis married."

Startled, Beau could only stare at his uncle, then, with gentle irony, he said, "You see too much."

He realized he hadn't thought of Julie, who'd been his paradigm for all womanhood, in comparison to Shelby even once. His cousin's wife belonged to another time, to a boy's ideal of the perfect woman.

"Yes," he said. "I'm over Julie."

The bittersweet passing of a youthful dream washed through him. He'd once thought of himself as a knight, riding forth on his white charger to right wrongs and to rescue fair maidens. Now he was a man and his needs were different—stronger, more demanding…and based on reality, one he found more intriguing than mere fantasies.

Chapter Nine

Shelby arrived at the clinic at six on Monday morning. Letting herself in the side door with the key Beau had given her, she went straight to the attic on the third floor. To her surprise, there were two rooms, both finished with white walls and hardwood floors. They looked as if they had never been used.

Except for the boxes and boxes of records stacked neatly on metal shelves usually found in garages and warehouses.

The chill of the night lingered in the rooms. She left the door open between the two spaces as she checked the dates on the records. At last she found one for the year she was born. Her heart went into warp speed.

She lowered the file box to the floor, sat and started going through the records. One by one, she searched through the medical histories, listing family names and births or deaths as she found them. At seven-thirty, she replaced the lid on the box, brushed the dust off her rear and returned to the first floor.

There had been a singular lack of pregnancies in the area during the year. Since her personal records indicated she'd been born in the hospital in South Carolina, she didn't know what she'd expected.

Washing up in the downstairs bathroom, she realized she'd hoped the doctor had seen a patient, perhaps a young, unmarried woman who was pregnant and that he'd referred her to a physician friend far from the area so she could have the child then return home with no one the wiser.

Shelby knew her birth mother had used the name Sandra Silvers and said she was a widow, but her adoptive parents were sure the information was false. They hadn't asked too many questions since they were glad to get the baby they had long awaited. The adoption was a private one through their family doctor.

Discouragement sat heavily on her shoulders as she donned a white jacket and checked the examining rooms for supplies before the day's routine began. The ringing of the old-fashioned doorbell interrupted her thoughts.

At the front door, she found a woman and a boy.

They looked Native American, the woman very old, the child no more than five or six.

"Good morning. It's a few minutes before the office opens, but you can come inside. Let's see, here's the sign-in sheet." She found the daily log on the clipboard in Bertie's office and held it out to the woman.

The elderly lady shook her head.

"You don't have an appointment?" Shelby asked.

"We came to see the doctor."

"He isn't in yet." She checked her watch. "The receptionist should be here in about twenty minutes. She can work you in or schedule an appointment."

The woman frowned. "I have someone waiting to take me home. Nicky, you will stay here and wait for your father. Be good. Don't cry." She patted the child on the shoulder.

The boy nodded.

With that, the woman turned and walked out.

"Wait!" Shelby called. She dashed from Bertie's desk, across the room and out onto the porch in record time. "You need to stay with the child."

"His father will take care of him."

"But...who is his father? When will he be here?"

"The doctor," the woman said, stopping by a pickup truck whose engine was running as if the driver was impatient to be off. "Dr. Dalton."

Shelby was stunned into silence.

The elderly woman got into the truck. "Nicky's grandmother, who was my sister, is dead. I don't know where his mother, my niece, is. She disappeared two years ago and has never returned. I am too old. The father will have to care for the son. It is only right.''

Before Shelby could reply to this news, the woman slammed the pickup door and the driver took off without giving them a chance for more conversation. Shelby took two steps forward, then realized it was hopeless.

Turning back, she spied a nylon bag by the door. She peered into the expressionless face of the boy, who silently observed the scene through the open door.

''Nicky?'' she said.

''Yes, ma'am,'' he said politely. His dark hair fell in an attractive sweep over his forehead. His eyes were a curious but fascinating combination of blue and brown.

''Nicky…Dalton?''

He stared at his feet. ''Nicholas Cloudwalker Jasper.''

Beau's first name was Nicholas, the same as his uncle Nick. ''Dr. Dalton is your father?''

He stared at her without speaking.

''Uh, perhaps you'd better wait in his office.'' She led the way to Beau's office, gave the child a couple of books and magazines appropriate for his age, and retreated to the side porch.

The doctor came out of the cottage, saw her, smiled and quickened his step. He joined her on the porch, took one look at her face and asked, "What's wrong? An emergency?"

She shook her head. "Not exactly."

When she said nothing else, he frowned. "You're beginning to worry me," he told her lightly. "Is it anything you can tell me about?"

"Uh, your son is in your office."

He appeared startled. "Come again?"

"Nicholas...Nicky...his great-aunt brought him. She said his grandmother is dead, that she doesn't know where his mother is, and she's too old to care for him."

His confusion seemed as great as her own. "Sorry, but I'm not getting any of this."

"The boy is in your office. Perhaps you'd better talk to him."

Giving her a look that indicated he thought one of them was crazy, he swept past her and disappeared inside. Ruth and Bertie arrived a couple of minutes later.

"Where's the doctor?" Bertie asked.

Shelby glanced at the closed office door. "In there. He, uh, might be a few minutes."

"Huh, we have a full schedule today."

"I'll weigh in the first patient and get her in the examining room, then..." She wasn't sure what came next.

"I hope he hasn't been cornered by a salesman," the receptionist muttered in annoyance. "If we start off behind, the day gets progressively worse."

Shelby called the first patient. "Hello, Mrs. Carter. How are you today?" she said, indicating the widow should step on the scale.

"That scale can't be right," the woman complained. "It always says I weigh five pounds more than the one at home."

Shelby smiled in sympathy. "I'll ask Dr. Dalton about the last time it was calibrated."

The patient nodded. When she was installed in the first examining room, her vital signs checked and recorded, Shelby went to the office. After a pause, she knocked lightly on the door.

"Patient in one," she said to let Beau know Mrs. Carter was ready for him.

"Shelby? Would you come in?"

She entered and closed the door behind her. The boy sat on the desk in front of Beau, who was in his chair.

"Nicky is going to stay in my office this morning," he said casually. "He'll be going to kindergarten for the afternoon session. Would you mind bringing him here after classes are over?"

"Not at all."

"Sorry to impose. I'll try to have other arrangements made tomorrow." He ran a hand through his hair as if not quite sure what those arrangements might be.

"Is...is...?" She realized she had no right to voice any questions. "Why don't I take him in with me when I go?" she volunteered.

He touched the boy's arm. "Miss Wheeling can stop by after we have lunch and take you to school this afternoon. Is that okay with you?" he asked the child, placing him in the chair and pushing it close to the desk.

Nicky looked from him to her. He nodded in his solemn way that grabbed at her heart. When she smiled, he did, too, but it was a cautious one, as if he'd learned not to expect too much.

She wondered how many times in his young life he'd been moved from one place to another. If his mother had left him with her mother and the grandmother had died, leaving him with the great-aunt, who had left him here, that meant there had been three major changes in his life.

The idea bothered her a great deal. Stability was important to a child. She'd been lucky at being settled with her adoptive parents at such an early age. Later, they'd stood by her when she'd desperately needed help.

"We'll talk tonight," Beau said, rising and leveling a steady gaze her way. "I'll explain things to Ruth and Bertie before they die of curiosity."

His smile was rather grim as he left the office.

The morning passed quickly. With three walk-ins with chicken pox, they were rushed to keep up. It was after twelve when Beau stopped her in the corridor. He handed her some money.

"Would you pick up something for Nicky for

lunch? Get yourself something, too. I'm not going to get a break.''

''Yes, I can handle it.''

He nodded, his attention already on the file in his hand as he walked toward his office. Nicky sat at the desk, coloring in a book from the children's waiting room. He'd been as quiet as a mouse all morning.

Pity squeezed her heart at the unusual patience for one so young. Anger simmered, too, at Beau, who had apparently left the mother to deal alone with the problem of pregnancy.

''I don't know much more about this than you do,'' Beau said sotto voce as he stopped at the door.

''Is he yours?''

He shrugged grimly. ''It's possible. I knew his mother in high school. We met again and dated briefly almost six years ago.''

Her eyes met his as she counted up the time and realized it fit the child's age.

''I was here on a visit after serving my internship. She knew where I was but didn't call when I moved to Boise and started my practice. I never thought about the possibility of a child.'' He stopped and shook his head.

The doubt in his eyes seemed genuine. Was it an act or was it real?

There was also the question of why the woman kept the baby a secret if it was Beau's child? Maybe she hadn't been sure whose it was, was one possible answer.

Looking at the solemn five-year-old, Shelby wondered how a mother could abandon her child. "What are you going to do?" she asked Beau.

"Damned if I know."

As he thrust back the lock that fell over his forehead, Shelby recalled the stubborn wave that swept attractively over his uncle's forehead, and also one of his cousins. She studied the child.

"Nicky has the same hairline and wave that a couple of your relatives have," she said. "And the blue in his eyes is the same shade as yours."

Beau narrowed his eyes as he, too, studied the child. "Should a youngster his age be so quiet?"

Other than to go to the bathroom—once she'd pointed out where it was—the boy hadn't left the office. He spoke only when spoken to. He was carefully polite.

"Maybe. It's according to his personality, but I think he's learned to keep a low profile."

"Yeah, I do, too."

At the look in his eyes, Shelby felt sorry for the mother or whoever had put fear into a child if Beau should ever catch up with them.

"Hey, champ," he said now, entering his office, "Shelby here is going to take you to lunch, then to school."

The blue-brown eyes went from the man, to her, and back without a blink.

He was used to being shifted among the adults in his life, she realized. Her heart filled with tears neither she nor the child would let fall. She smiled at him. "I'm the school nurse, so I'll be there all afternoon, too. I'll bring you home after the classes are over. You ready to go?"

Nicky nodded, rose, carefully closed the coloring book and put the crayons in their box, then came to her. She took his hand.

"Here's money for lunch," Beau told her, holding out a twenty.

She declined the money. "We'll eat at my place. It's quieter. Then we'll head on over to the school."

"Thanks. I owe you one."

"Not me," she said softly. "Maybe him." She nodded to the boy.

"Yeah. I guess I'd better call Seth and find out what to do. And see about a sitter."

Shelby nodded and led Nicky out to her car. At her house, they decided grilled cheese sandwiches with tomatoes were a good choice. The fact that she gave the child a choice seemed to floor him for a second before he shyly indicated his preference by pointing at the package of cheese in her left hand rather than the peanut butter jar in her right.

During the meal, she talked about the flowers around the cottage and how much she enjoyed the lake. She invited him to join her on her afternoon walk. He nodded.

At school, he led her to his classroom. Leaving him on a bench nearby, she talked to the teacher. The grandmother had enrolled him last spring and put herself down as his guardian. Since classes had started, a neighbor had been bringing Nicky to school when he delivered his own child.

Shelby decided she had better let Beau handle the change in caretaker and any explanation he decided to give. She told the teacher she would pick Nicky up at three.

Going to the boy, she knelt in front of him and told him she would come for him. She held his hand while she spoke and felt his fingers tighten on hers for a second before he let go and staunchly marched into the classroom by himself as the bell rang.

In the school office, she checked Nicky's records for additional information, but found nothing new, only the grandmother's name and address as the next of kin.

Shortly before three, she called the clinic and told Bertie she was taking Nicky home with her until the office closed, then she would bring him by.

"I'll tell the doctor," Bertie promised. She lowered her voice. "I think he's still in a state of shock. So are Ruth and I, for that matter." She laughed wryly. "This will entertain the local gossips for weeks."

"I'm sure," Shelby murmured, then said goodbye as the final bell rang. She locked the office and hurried to the kindergarten classroom.

Even for a shy child, Nicky seemed too quiet. He was almost listless. Automatically reaching over after they were belted into her car, she felt his forehead. Hot. She was positive he had a fever.

"Let's go to the clinic and check your temperature," she said. "Are you feeling ill?"

He hesitated, then shook his head.

She wasn't sure whether to believe him or not. He seemed a terribly stoic child. Again she experienced the pressure of tears inside and was reminded of her own baby, who had grown too weak to cry or even smile at the end.

"Here we are," she said with forced cheer when they arrived at the offices.

Going in the side door, she spoke to Bertie, then took Nicky into Beau's office. There, she checked his temperature and found it was indeed elevated four degrees above normal.

After leaving him with a cup of apple juice and some snack crackers, she checked to see if Beau was free. He wasn't. She waited in the hall until he exited the examining room.

"What is it?" he asked at once upon seeing her.

"Nicky. He's running a fever. Four degrees."

"Chicken pox?"

"Probably. His throat isn't sore, and there's no tummy ache or flu symptoms."

"The health department reported we now have over twenty cases at this end of the county. Almost all the kids had the vaccine through county services. They're investigating."

She nodded. "After you see Nicky, I thought I'd take him to your place until you're through here."

He touched her lightly on the shoulder. "I guess

I'll owe you two now,'' he joked, then shook his head and headed for his next appointment.

After Nicky's examination, Shelby took the child to the tiny cottage. He lay on the sofa while she rummaged through his bag for a pair of pajamas. None was there, but she did find a birth certificate with a social security card stapled to it.

Beau was listed as Nicky's father, but the mother had given the child her own last name. Because of not being married, or did that matter? Shelby had no idea of the law that governed these matters.

She found a pitcher of tea in the small refrigerator and prepared a glass, then she sat on the tiny porch and waited. One by one the cars disappeared from the parking lot of the clinic until only Bertie's vehicle remained, along with Beau's pickup. Then only the pickup was there.

It was after six before he came down the flagstone path to the tiny house. ''Amelia is sending over some salads and soup from the B and B. I thought we could have supper here,'' he said. ''Is he sleeping?''

''Yes. I just checked on him. He's cooler, I think.''

''Good. He'll be broken out by morning, but it should be a light case. I've got a couple of calls out for a sitter. Bertie and Ruth are checking, too.''

He smiled a bit grimly. Worry was indicated by twin vertical lines etched between the black eyebrows.

''Uncle Nick volunteered to take over Nicky's care.

He wants me to bring the boy out to the ranch. But his catching chicken pox is the last thing I need.''

They heard a car outside. Beau went to greet the visitor and returned with two plastic bags. Inside was the promised food from the B and B owner, plus assorted muffins and homemade rolls. They ate on the porch while Nicky continued to sleep.

''The sleep of the innocent,'' Beau said, looking at his son after they stored the rest of the meal in the kitchen.

''I suspect he hasn't slept well since his grandmother died. It's unsettling for a child not to know where he belongs—'' She stopped upon realizing her words could be taken as a criticism.

''You're right,'' Beau agreed. ''He must be feeling abandoned by everyone he's ever known.''

''Yes, well, I should be going.''

''Stay for a while longer, just till he wakes up. He seems to trust you.''

They returned to the porch with glasses of iced tea and watched the shadows grow long across the lawn.

''What will you do about him?'' she asked, voicing a concern that had grown steadily with the passing of time.

He sighed. ''To tell the truth, I'm not sure. Seth said he would check everything out A.S.A.P. There was a copy of the birth certificate in the bag. I'm listed as the father.''

''I, uh, saw it when I was looking for pajamas. Why doesn't Nicky have your last name?''

"You would have to ask his mother about that. I sure haven't been able to figure out her thinking."

Shelby was silent.

Beau continued. "I tried to call the aunt, but she wasn't home. Or she wasn't answering the phone. She lives on a small ranch outside of town, apparently alone. Bertie says the husband died a few years ago and the son hasn't been around in years. She and her sister, Nicky's grandmother, were the last of the original Cloudwalker family."

"And Nicky's mother," Shelby added.

"Her name was Elena Jasper. Seth and Zack are trying to find out what happened to her."

"I can't imagine a mother leaving—"

"Her child?" he finished when she stopped abruptly.

Hearing a noise, she glanced at the door. Nicky stood there, silent and watchful.

"Hi," she said. "You must be hungry."

"I itch," he told her, not looking at his father.

Beau followed her inside, and they both checked the child. Ten small blisters dotted his face. That many more were on his chest.

"I have something at the office for that itch," he said. "I'll go get it."

After he left, Nicky turned to her. "Is he really my daddy?"

She glanced toward the door, but Beau was nowhere in sight. "That's what it says on your birth certificate."

The shy smile appeared. "I always wanted one. Nana said she was going to take me to see him, but she got sick and didn't feel like it."

"Did she say where your mother was?"

He nodded. "I forget, though."

"Well, that's okay. If you remember, you can tell me or your daddy."

A frown knit the young face. "She didn't come home for my birthday like she said she would."

The sad resignation in his tone was almost more than Shelby could bear. A five-year-old should never be that disappointed in life. "I see," she said, and tried to think of a reason for the failure to appear.

He supplied one. "Maybe she was sick. Maybe she had chicken pox, too."

"Maybe," Shelby said, resisting the urge to hold him tightly so that nothing could hurt him again. Why did the young and innocent have to suffer?

Beau returned with a tube of medicine and rubbed it on the spots, then provided a T-shirt for Nicky to sleep in. She noted how gently he worked with the child and how Nicky instinctively reacted to the gentleness.

In time father and son would come to know each other. Trust would grow along with companionship. As if she could see into the future, she knew Nicky would grow into a fine young man under his father's care.

Shelby heated a bowl of soup and brought it to the coffee table. Beau put a cushion on the floor and had the boy sit there to eat. Nicky, she noted, became silent once more. She wondered if the boy was afraid of the man.

She also wondered what it said about Beau that Nicky's mother hadn't contacted him about the coming child. A man of callous indifference didn't fit with the nurturing ways she observed in him. So why didn't the woman go to him?

No answers came to her then, nor shortly after, when she returned to the cottage by the lake.

Chapter Ten

Shelby worked in the attic records, sorting through another box, then bringing it down with her to run through the shredder. Finished, she washed up and donned a jacket, then found Beau and Nicky in his office.

"No luck with a sitter," Beau explained. "He'll be contagious until all the blisters crust over, so we'll have to keep him isolated."

Shelby dropped to her haunches in front of the child. He gave her his tentative smile. She brushed the wave off his forehead. "Did you sleep okay last night?"

Nicky leaned forward to whisper, "After…" He glanced at Beau, then leaned close again. "After *he* put the medicine on again."

She realized Nicky didn't know what to call Beau. "Good. No school for you today. I'll tell your teacher. I rented a couple of videos from the market. Have you seen *Beauty and the Beast*?"

"No, ma'am."

"My name is Shelby. You can call me that, okay?"

Leaving him in the office with the door partially closed, she and Beau washed up in preparation for the first patient.

"Nicky doesn't know what to call you," she told him, using the brush under her nails and passing it to him.

"That makes two of us."

At the grumpy tone, she looked him over, noting the fatigue around his eyes. "Did you sleep last night?"

"Not well. I'm not used to sleeping on the floor." His smile was sardonic.

"Oh. You'll have to get a cot or something for Nicky."

"I've already called the furniture store for a roll-away. The owner suggested a trundle that will roll under the daybed for easy storage. He's going to bring it out today."

"Good." She finished washing and dried her hands. "Do you want Nicky to call you 'daddy' or by your name?"

His gaze probed hers. "Sounds as if you've made up your mind that he's mine."

She realized that was true. "I'm sorry. You're

right. I was making an assumption from seeing the birth certificate. And there are similarities to your family.''

''It's okay. I think he is, too. From the information with his birth certificate, we have the same blood type, and the timing of the birth is right.'' He shrugged as if accepting this evidence as proof.

Her hesitation was brief. ''Then you need to tell him you are his father...and what you want to be called.''

A smile slowly dawned on his handsome face. ''It seems strange, but I guess 'daddy' is about right, don't you?''

She couldn't keep the smile of approval off her face. ''Yes, for a five-year-old. Around ten or so, most kids shorten it to 'dad.'''

''I've never thought of myself as a parent. I guess I'll have to mend my wicked ways and become a model citizen.'' He inhaled deeply and let it out in an audible whoosh, as if relieved at making a major decision. ''Okay, Nurse, you ready to greet our first patient?''

''Yes, Doctor,'' she said primly, feeling a mysterious glow inside, as if a lamp had been turned on.

At school that afternoon she reported Nicky's absence to the office and his teacher, then went to the nursing station and answered several calls, mostly on the duration of chicken pox. She couldn't believe the children had had their shots although the parents said they had.

She and a sixth-grader had a long talk about the birds and bees when the girl began her menses and burst into tears. Shelby spoke matter-of-factly about the changes in life that people went through and the emotional uncertainty thus produced. They discussed growth and the fears and the excitement that went along with it.

A boy fell and split his chin on the asphalt. Shelby applied ice, then a butterfly bandage and called the parents to suggest they check with their doctor about stitches.

At three, she realized she was tired. She'd planned on returning to the clinic and taking Nicky to Beau's cottage, now she paused to reconsider the decision. Perhaps she was getting too involved with Beau and his newly found family.

But Nicky would need a break from being confined in the office most of the day. Thinking of him, she drove to the clinic. Her heart pounded furiously when she went inside.

"He's taking a nap at the house," Beau told her, stopping in the hall when he spotted her at his office door. "Bertie's niece is staying with him."

There was no need to be disappointed, she scolded herself at this news. She was hardly indispensable.

"I told her to bring him back up here at three-thirty. She has to leave then."

Shelby glanced at her watch. It was three-twenty. "I can stay with him at the house. He was probably getting claustrophobic in the office."

"That's what I thought, too." He touched her shoulder, then withdrew. "Thanks for seeing me through this. I've been in a daze since yesterday."

His gaze fastened on her mouth. For a second she thought she saw need as well as gratitude in those depths, then he blinked and continued with his duties.

She went to the cottage where Nicky slept.

The teenager was glad to be relieved. "Tell Dr. Dalton I can stay from one until three-thirty tomorrow, too. I have classes in the morning, then work at the drugstore in the evening," she explained.

Shelby nodded. "I can take over when school is out each afternoon, so between us, we'll manage fine."

Alone, she sat on the porch and leafed through a medical journal. The temperature was in the high seventies. Bees droned among the clover scattered in the lawn. At last, she kicked her shoes off, curled up on the wicker settee and fell asleep.

Beau stood outside the cottage, a smile tugging at his mouth as he observed the two occupants through the screen door. Shelby and Nicky were playing a board game with the quiet intensity of a master chess tournament. They seemed to hit it off with each other.

A surprising combination of hunger and contentment spread through him. He wasn't used to having anyone at his place when he arrived home, either here or in Boise.

It was…nice.

Like the lights coming up on a stage, he recalled another time, another house. He'd been a boy then, Roni a baby. His mother had been nursing Roni and humming a soft melody while he'd read aloud from a favorite book. His dad had been watching the news on television.

His parents had assumed he'd memorized the book—and he had—but he could also identify easy words in other books.

"This boy is bound for college," his father had said, tossing him into the air so that he'd nearly bumped the ceiling when they realized he could read. "He's going to be an educated man, not a rodeo bum like his old man."

It was that moment, Beau realized, that his future had been sealed. College had become his fate. His mother had died the next year, his dad in the avalanche when he was eight. He'd learned about scholarships, earned one, then paid for everything else through summer construction jobs.

He'd been determined to live up to his parents' expectations for him.

Time shifted forward and hc was twenty-five. He'd finished all his training and was home on a visit. Elena had been home that spring, too. Travis and Julie had married, and Elena had gone to the wedding as his date. They'd seen each other for six weeks before he'd moved to Boise and begun work.

From that brief liaison, they had apparently produced a child—as difficult as that was to believe;

she'd been on birth control pills. He wondered what his expectations for his own son should be, what tenets he should try to impart to a child growing up in today's world.

He looked at the silken fall of Shelby's flaming hair and the near-black locks of the boy. If they had met years ago, Nicky could have been their child. Together they would have figured out how to raise him—

"Oh, hi," Shelby said, glancing up and seeing him. "You're just in time. This young man is beating the socks off me."

Beau's insides tightened when Nicky smothered a laugh behind his hand. He remembered laughing as a child, a full-throated shout of delight while playing with his dad.

His dad's twin brother had always been around, too, so it was like having two fathers, plus he and Roni had grown up with their cousins. One big, happy family. It had been the same living at the ranch with Uncle Nick.

This quiet five-year-old had never experienced that kind of family and sense of belonging. He realized that was the heritage he wanted to give his son.

His son. That fact still stunned his senses.

He thawed chicken in the microwave oven, then grilled it while the other two finished their game. Shelby made the salad and nuked potatoes before bringing them out to brown on the grill while the chicken cooked.

With only two dining chairs inside, they opted to sit on the porch and share the coffee table there. He and Shelby sat on the short wicker sofa while Nicky knelt on the floor across the low table from them, silent now that *he* was home.

After the dishes were done, Nicky whispered to Shelby. She spoke to Beau. "Nicky would like to watch *Beauty and the Beast* again. Do you mind?"

"Not at all. I haven't seen it."

This obviously surprised her.

"I've been busy," he said. "Videos weren't in my budget while I was at medical school."

She wrinkled her nose at him, which made him think of kissing her. "Mine, either," she told him. "I could barely keep my head above water in nursing school."

When she hesitated, he knew she was recalling the past. "Did you take the four-year course so you earned a college degree as well as your R.N.?" he asked to distract her.

"Yes. I worked night shift and did extra work during the day to be certified in pediatrics."

He prepared microwave popcorn and they settled in to watch the animated musical. When he laughed at the villain's swaggering song and dance routine, he was gratified to hear Nicky join in. When he looked, Shelby was smiling, her gaze on them. He liked having her approval.

Heat bubbled through his blood as their eyes met. He wanted her with a hunger deeper than any he'd ever experienced. When she wasn't with him, he found himself wondering where she was and what she was doing. When they worked together, it was with mutual respect and an ease that surprised him. When they kissed, her passion matched his.

His affair with Nicky's mother had been one of mutual restlessness—she from breaking up with a long-time boyfriend, he at the marriage of his cousin to the woman he'd been half in love with for years.

With Shelby, nothing else entered into it. They were simply a man and a woman who struck sparks off each other.

"I'd better go," she said, standing as soon as the movie was over.

"Stay for a glass of wine," he invited. "After we get this young man to bed."

He stood back and let her supervise as Nicky washed up and brushed his teeth. After the anti-itch cream was spread over the bumps and the T-shirt was on, Beau pulled out the trundle bed and covered his son with the sheet.

"I'll add the blanket later, when it cools down."

"It was forty-two degrees this morning when I got up," she told him. "Winter will be here before we know it."

"You've been coming in early. How's it going on the old files?" He poured them each a glass of white wine and followed her to the porch.

Catching her hand when she would have sat in the

rather flimsy old wooden chair, he escorted her to the sofa and tugged her down beside him.

"The moon is rising," he said.

She turned to where he pointed. Her lips were close to his...temptingly close.

"I can't resist," he said, an apology and a warning.

He kissed her then, just his lips on hers, no hands, no body contact, nothing to make it hard for her to pull away.

She stayed.

Heat poured through him like lava bursting from the vent of a volcano, drowning him in the wild, urgent hunger. Without losing contact, he set the wineglass down and ran his fingers into her silky-smooth hair. Her scent enclosed him. He half smiled as he realized she was as hot as he was.

When she at last eased away, he murmured, "That was good. As good as it gets."

She shook her head.

"Yes."

"There are so many complications," she said, her voice delightfully husky.

He realized she wasn't denying the passion between them, but that other things—his son, a miscarriage or possibly a child from her past, the mistakes they'd both made, the hesitation they both felt as the hunger grew stronger—all these combined to make her wary.

He reluctantly let her go. "I know." Settling back in the glider and setting it to gently swinging, he added, "I'll have someone in for Nicky tomorrow. Bertie has a friend who's agreed to come over as long as I need her."

Shelby nodded, her expression unreadable in the faint moonlight.

He laughed ruefully. "That's probably for the best. We can't do much on a porch or in a bed with a five-year-old sleeping beside it."

She made a slight sound.

"Next time we're alone..." He let the thought trail off, but it was a promise. He thought of the rooms above the clinic. There were at least four empty bedrooms on the second floor.

This time she did gasp. Leaping to her feet, nearly spilling the wine in her haste to escape, she muttered about an early day tomorrow and ran for the door.

He walked her to the parking lot and saw her off. They were at a stalemate at present, but they had the rest of the school year to work out the situation between them. That was a whole nine months.

Going back inside, he studied the sleeping child.

His?

On a gut level, he knew it was true. The way the boy's hair formed a wave that fell over his forehead was just like Uncle Nick's. His eyes were mostly Dalton blue, but with those curious brown flecks around the iris, as if his mother's genes had insisted on having some influence.

Nicky was also tall for his age and as skinny as all the Daltons had been as kids.

Yeah. There was enough visible evidence to indicate paternity. Now if he could just figure out how to
be a father to a five-year-old.

Beau smiled. Uncle Nick could tell him a thing or
two, and most likely would do so. He'd take Nicky
out to the ranch, come the weekend.

On Tuesday a week later, Shelby finished shred-
ding the contents of the file folders. The folders were
old and yellowed, the paper becoming fragile. Those
she stacked in a trash bag to take to the recycling
center.

Finally she picked up the folder she'd laid aside.
In it was information she was interested in. A man
by the name of Ralph Silvers had been treated by the
old doctor for an injury associated with a mining operation. The date was one that would coincide with
the month of her conception.

Silvers was the name her birth mother had used.
Maybe it hadn't been false, after all. Maybe they had
been married… But why go away and have the baby
in that case?

Maybe he'd died before they could be married.

Shelby frowned as she put the record in her purse
and discarded the folder. She was grasping at straws,
but there was one person who might be able to tell
her something.

At the next Historical Society meeting to discuss
their research findings, she would ask the retired

teacher if she'd known Silvers. Perhaps Miss Pickford had had him as a student. In fact, it was likely.

From the record, Ralph Silvers had been twenty-two at the time of the accident. Old enough to be a father.

There had to be a clue in all this—the bracelet made in the area that had prompted her to come here to begin her search, the name used by her birth mother and the fact that she'd been twenty-one, a year younger than the miner with the same last name who had definitely been here at the right time.

In her bones, Shelby felt a deep connection to this place, as if all that she was had originated here in this high valley so far off the beaten path.

"Finished?" Bertie asked when she left the room containing the copier, shredder and other business machines.

"Yes. I'm heading for home and a shower. It's amazing how dusty things get from sitting around."

"Huh. You should live on a gravel road like I do, then you would really see dust."

Beau exited his office. He yawned and stretched. "Man, I'm beat. You want to join us for dinner?"

"Sorry," Bertie said, "but I have a date. I know, why don't you invite Shelby instead?"

Beau gave his receptionist a severe frown while Shelby smiled. When the older woman left them to answer the phone, he raised his eyebrows at Shelby.

She shook her head. "I, uh, have things to do."

At present she wasn't in the mood for small talk

and the hot undercurrents that ran between her and the handsome doctor every minute they were together.

"How's Nicky?" she asked. "I saw him in school today, but from a distance. I didn't get a chance to speak."

"He's fine. He likes the sitter we found, but she's not as much fun as you, he says. I agree."

Like magnets, her eyes were drawn to his. He devoured her on the spot with a visual hunger so strong it made her tremble. If they'd been alone, she wouldn't have been able to resist the temptation of his kiss.

"I have to go," she said, and fled his dynamic presence. She needed to think, and it was impossible around him.

Shelby finished her swim across the narrow reservoir lake and back. Crossing the lawn to the cottage, she said hello to Nicky and two older boys she recognized from the elementary school. They were taking turns at bat while the others pitched or fielded the balls.

It was Saturday afternoon, and Beau and Zack were wrapping the walls of the lodge with a layer of plastic sheeting as protection against wind and rain. A crew of men crawled over the roof, which was now on, like busy ants, nailing black felt into place. She nodded to those who looked her way, then went inside.

After a quick shower, she dried her hair, pulled on

black slacks and a black-and-white floral print top and went out on the porch to read the paper.

"He's not your dad," she heard one of the boys say.

"He is, too."

That was Nicky. She recognized his voice.

"You don't have the same last name," one of the older boys said, his tone a verbal sneer of disbelief.

"That's 'cause I have my mom's," Nicky replied.

The first boy spoke up. "Yeah. She wasn't married to Dr. Dalton, so he couldn't be your dad."

"Yes, he is. My nana said so."

Shelby's insides clenched at the stoic defense and the hint of tears in Nicky's voice.

"So why didn't you ever live with him?"

"Because I lived with my mom. Lots of kids don't live with their dads." He named another child as an example.

"His dad is dead," the first kid scoffed.

"No, he isn't." Nicky's voice was assured now. "He lives in Nevada. He came to school and showed us some gold and stuff he found."

Having no argument to this, the older boys decided they had to return to the R.V. resort, owned by their parents, on the other side of the lake. They raced off. Nicky went down to the shore and built a tiny fort with rocks.

Shelby sighed and settled back in the chair. It had been two weeks since the great-aunt had left Nicky at the clinic. The child was still quiet, especially around his father. She pondered the idea of speaking to Beau about the older boys taunting Nicky. Before she could decide, her musing was interrupted.

"Hi. Nicky and I are on our way over to the restaurant. Care to join us for a treat?" Beau stopped outside the screen door and waited for her answer.

She nodded. She would think on the walk over to the Crow's Nest. "Let me get some shoes on."

Slipping into sandals, she joined the two Daltons on the trail. Nicky ran in front of them. At the dam, he peered over the edge, looking for fish, while he waited for them to catch up.

"He's adjusting to being with you," she said.

Beau nodded. "I showed him the ranch last weekend. Uncle Nick took to him like the proverbial lost son. I think Nicky was pretty impressed at having so many relatives. Roni and Seth came up from the city and we had a big welcoming dinner, complete with chocolate cake and ice cream."

"That was a wonderful thing to do." She hesitated, wondering if now was the time to bring up the problem Nicky was having about his name. Frowning, she chided herself that it was none of her business—

"Go ahead and say whatever is on your mind."

She blinked at Beau, then realized her worry must have shown on her face. "The two boys who were over earlier were, uh, questioning Nicky's parentage. They didn't believe you were his father since you don't have the same last name."

Beau uttered a low curse.

"Nicky had an answer." She related the conversation she'd overheard. "Are you...is there anything you can do, like adopt him or get his birth certificate changed or something?" Another thought came to her. "Are you going to have DNA testing done to see if he is yours?"

Beau shook his head. "I've accepted that he is. So has the family. Seth will handle getting the records changed. And since I am listed as his father on his birth certificate, there will be no custody issues."

"Good. Nicky has been through enough in his young life." She clamped her mouth shut. She had no say in the child's fate. Except she had thought of adoption if no one wanted him.

"I agree." Beau took her arm as they crossed the road over the dam. Nicky walked a few feet in front of them.

"The health department called," she remembered to tell him. "The chicken pox vaccine supplied by the drug company was ineffective. It was diluted to the point that there was no immunity produced."

"That's what I suspected."

"The company has launched a full investigation and will supply free antiviral medication and vaccine to the county."

"Good," he said.

Shelby saw the two boys who had played with Nicky earlier helping a man arrange rocks around a flower bed.

"Wait up," Beau called to Nicky and held out a hand. "I want you to meet some friends."

Leading the way, Beau introduced Shelby to the park owner and his sons. "And this is my son, Nicky. He's living with me now."

Shelby saw Nicky glance at his father, then stare down at his shoes. After the boys mumbled a greeting, Beau invited them over to play again sometime and thanked them for including Nicky in their game earlier. After chatting a minute more, he escorted his two companions to the restaurant for ice cream sundaes.

Over the treat, Beau asked Nicky if he wanted to go by Jasper or Dalton. "It's up to you," he ended casually.

"Dalton," Nicky said in a barely audible voice.

"Fine. Isn't this the best hot fudge you ever ate?" Beau demanded, scooping up a big bite.

And just that easily, he solved Nicky's problem with his name and parentage. Shelby's heart went as warm and oozy as the hot fudge.

Beau leaned close. "Keep looking at me like that and I'll be forced to kiss you senseless."

Nicky giggled.

"I'll tell your uncle Nick," she warned.

"Hey, don't you remember his advice about the seduction and all that? You're not doing your part there."

Her glance went to the child.

"I've been thinking about furnishing the bedrooms

over the clinic. Nicky and I are going to need a little privacy pretty soon.''

''I can move,'' she immediately volunteered, ''so you can enlarge the cottage the way you'd planned.''

He shook his head. ''I've got to get the clinic paid for first. Since the drug company will make good on the vaccine, maybe the county will forget that thousand buck pledge,'' he added, so ruefully it was clear he didn't think this was really a possibility.

''Dream on,'' she advised with a laugh.

''Yeah,'' he said, looking at her, letting her know what was in his dreams.

Her own dreams had been confusing of late. In them, a man, standing in a mist that hid his face, told her he couldn't stay. He would turn and leave. Sometimes she heard a child crying in the dream; sometimes she knew it was her baby, but other times she wasn't sure. It could have been her.

Heading to her car, she wondered where this quest she felt compelled to follow was going to lead. Not to happiness, she thought, and felt the loneliness of the past ten years wash over her.

Chapter Eleven

"I've written a brief history of the Native American origins in the area in the first chapter," Miss Pickford explained on the following Wednesday. "Then in the second chapter, I added the European trappers and ended with the Lewis and Clark expedition opening the West to settlement. The third chapter will begin with the first ranchers."

"We know who filed the first land claims," Amelia said, waving her list.

"And I have the records of the mining claims," the other member of their group said.

When Miss Pickford looked her way, Shelby nodded and indicated the papers she held. "I found the files from the old doctor's earliest years. Most of the names correlate to the family names Amelia found."

The leader of the group was pleased. "Since the paper ran the article on our project, I've received several letters detailing family histories, including information on private burial grounds. So far, so good."

After the discussion was concluded and the meeting declared officially over, Shelby scanned the list of mining claims. Her heart lurched when she noted the name Ralph Silvers among them.

"If a person found gold or valuable ore on a claim, would there be a record of it?" she asked.

"There could be," Miss Pickford said, perusing the sheet of mining claims Shelby held. "Through the old assay office files."

"Where are they kept?"

"In Council, possibly, or down in Boise."

The records at the county seat would be easy enough to check, Shelby decided. If she found nothing there, she would find out where to go in Boise and plan a trip there on the next teachers' workday when the students would be off.

After the two older women left, Shelby and Amelia had lunch. Honey Dalton came in just as they were finishing.

"Join us," Amelia invited. "Iced tea? Have you had lunch?"

Honey blotted her face on a towel draped on her shoulder. "Just tea, please." She plopped into a chair next to Shelby while Amelia went to the kitchen. "How's the clinic going?" she asked.

"Busy," Shelby said. "Beau is thinking of opening on Wednesday as well as Saturday morning." She grimaced. "I like having the morning off for shopping and chores."

Honey's flushed face took on a worried aspect. "He already works at least ten hours a day the other days of the week, plus Saturday morning. Uncle Nick thinks that's enough. Last weekend he got after Zack about taking time for family when he was late for Nicky's welcoming party."

"I see your husband working on the resort lodge a lot," Shelby said. "In addition to being a deputy, doesn't he also raise and train cutting horses?"

"Yes. I'm learning to help with the horses. It's fun." Honey's smile flashed, then she looked worried again. "We bought twenty acres a mile up from the new lodge and plan to renovate the house there next year, if all goes well."

"That sounds wonderful," Shelby said sincerely, and tried not to feel envious.

"The dance studio is doing better than I thought it would. I'm trying to talk Zack and his brothers into hiring a contractor for the house, but they want to do everything themselves. They barely got Travis's house finished before the wedding."

"Speaking of the studio, Beau suggested we look into doing some kind of exercise class that he can prescribe to his patients. I would weigh them in and monitor their heart rate if you would plan a routine to music. Have you considered something like that?"

Honey shook her head. When she laughed, Shelby

gave her a questioning glance. "It's never dull around the Dalton gang," she explained. "They always have a dozen ideas going at once. It appears you and I have been recruited for the latest brainstorm."

Amelia returned. "Sorry. I got a call about a late delivery from one of our suppliers. What's your latest brainstorm?"

"Not mine," Honey corrected. "Beau's. He thinks we should add exercise classes at the studio."

"That's a wonderful idea." Amelia placed a tall glass of iced tea in front of the dance instructor and refilled Shelby's glass. "I could use some exercise myself. Marta's scones are too tempting to resist."

After discussing the pros and cons of the idea, Honey asked about the chicken pox epidemic. Shelby told them it seemed to be winding down and had been traced to an ineffective batch of vaccine. She checked the time.

"I have to report in to the school. Thanks for lunch," she said to Amelia, and left with Honey's promise to think about the exercise class.

At school, she weighed in Kenisha, checked with the girl on taking a daily vitamin and noted the weight gain on the girl's record. After the disastrous start of the school year with the chicken pox, everything seemed to be settling into a standard routine of head and tummy aches, a few allergies to the fall-blooming weeds and a few scrapes on the playground, mostly among the younger children.

At three, Shelby locked the office, reported the

day's incidents to the principal and left. She drove immediately to the county seat to check the records before the courthouse closed. An hour later she had the address in Lost Valley where Ralph Silvers once lived and the location of his mining claim in the mountains west of town.

The next day, she researched the name with the local newspaper archives. Silvers had found gold on his claim and, from his remarks to the reporter, apparently thought he had struck it rich. Unfortunately the quartz vein containing the mineral was shallow and was mined out in a couple of months, according to a later article.

On Saturday morning, instead of her usual jog and walk by the lake, she explored a side street in the town. There she stopped in front of a Victorian home that looked as if it had been built in the late eighteen hundreds.

The house was in good condition, with a nice lawn and lots of flowering borders. Her father—if that's who he was—had boarded there. He'd worked for a copper mining operation before making his own claim and finding gold.

"Good morning," a familiar voice said behind her.

Miss Pickford of the Historical Society stood at the edge of the lawn next door. Shelby returned the greeting.

"Is that your house?" she asked. "It's lovely."

"Yes. Thank you," the spinster replied. "It was built in 1889 and has been in my family since that time. My cousin lived next door." She indicated the house where Ralph Silvers had once lived. "She ran a boarding house."

Envy, sharp and poignant, ran over Shelby. Miss Pickford spoke with such surety, her knowledge of her roots giving her an inherent confidence that could be taken for arrogance or snobbery when, Shelby was sure, none was intended.

"How nice to have family next door," Shelby said, wondering how she could lead in to the questions that swarmed through her head. "Does your cousin still live there?"

"She died years ago. Her daughter sold the place to a couple from Boise who use it for a vacation home."

"Oh." Shelby looked into the blue eyes that seemed to see right through her. For a second, Shelby considered Miss Pickford as a possibility for her birth mother, but that was far-fetched. The former teacher was surely too old.

Another idea came to her. "Your cousin's daughter, did she grow up here? Was she a student of yours?"

Miss Pickford's smile was dry. "Most people in this end of the county were students of mine at one time or another."

"Of course," Shelby said. She studied the neat Victorian house next door. "I think I would want to live in a home like that rather than sell it. Does the daughter live on a ranch around here?"

Shelby wanted to ask the daughter's name, but couldn't think of a way to bring it up that would sound natural. The seconds passed while Miss Pickford studied her. A sheen of nervous perspiration swept over Shelby as she wondered if she'd already been too inquisitive.

"No. She married a minister. He retired five years ago and they moved to Arizona because of his arthritis. They were both killed in a car accident shortly after that."

The disappointment was so keen Shelby had to press a hand to her chest. Another dead end. "I was reading about the mining claims in the newspaper archives. A man named Silvers, the one who found gold, boarded with your cousin. What happened to him and the claim when it didn't pan out?"

"He left and never came back. He wasn't from around here. You've certainly been a help to us on the local history project," the former teacher said. She looked at the mountain peaks, her gaze distant and thoughtful. "Sometimes I wonder if it isn't better to let the past stay buried."

Then her gaze returned to Shelby.

Alarm jangled through Shelby's nerves. She wondered if this was some kind of subtle warning to forget the past and let it be. Miss Pickford had studied the copper bracelet closely and known its value. She'd known Ralph Silvers, too, or at least something of him while he boarded next door.

Could Ralph have been her father? Had he seduced

some young woman with his dreams of getting rich? Perhaps the cousin. No, she would have been older than twenty-one at the time. Maybe the daughter. No, she was older than the fifty-one or fifty-two necessary to be her mother since she and her husband had been old enough to retire.

Unless she'd married an older man?

Looking at Miss Pickford's closed expression, Shelby didn't think this was the time to ask, but she did have one more question.

"None of the daughter's children was interested in keeping their ancestral home?" She gazed at the house as if envious of having such a heritage.

Shelby didn't think the older woman was going to answer, but she finally said, "Unfortunately, she and her husband had no children."

"Oh, that's too bad. Well, I'd better get on with my exercise," Shelby said with forced cheer. "Nice talking to you." With a wave, she headed on down the street at a jog.

She could hardly wait to get to the newspaper office to check out the minister who had retired five years ago. There would surely be a notice of the tragedy of the car wreck in the obituary column.

The newspaper office was closed, she found. She'd have to wait until Monday for further information. She returned to the cottage. Beau arrived when she did. He wore jeans and a work shirt.

"Hi," he called as she paused by the back door.

"Hi." She studied his attire. "It seems odd for the local doctor to moonlight as a construction worker."

His grin went right down to her toes. "It's good exercise. When the lodge is finished, I'll have to do something else. Maybe I'll join you."

She thought of early morning walks with him. Other things they could do came to mind. "Uh, where's Nicky?"

"Zack took him out to the ranch for the weekend." The deep blue eyes seemed to go darker. "How about dinner tonight?"

She tried desperately to think of something she had to do. Not a thing came to mind. She nodded, then quickly went inside, her heart beating way too fast. She knew she shouldn't have accepted the invitation, but want far outweighed sense, she found.

In the shower she reasoned that she wouldn't be in the area forever, so what difference did it make if she and the handsome doctor were involved for a short time? If she was careful and didn't allow herself to fall in love, then it should bc okay. She was an adult. She could handle passion.

An icy tremor produced chill bumps all the way down her back in spite of the warm water sluicing over her. She suddenly wasn't very sure of her ability to handle anything. Neither was she sure she really wanted to find her past. She knew, as well as anyone, how painful it could be.

Was that what Miss Pickford had meant in her

warning about leaving it buried? Did the retired teacher have her own painful memories of a love gone wrong?

Beau arrived at seven with two steaks, rolls, a bag of salad greens and a bottle of wine. He wore fresh jeans and a white shirt. His hair was damp from a recent shower.

"I come bearing gifts," he said, his gaze sweeping over her appreciatively. "I thought we could grill the steaks. You got a couple of potatoes we can zap in the microwave?"

Shelby nodded. She wore red slacks with a white shirt. Like him, she'd rolled the shirt sleeves up. A red, white and blue scarf held her hair off her face.

While he started the grill on the screened porch, she washed two potatoes and put them in the microwave oven to cook. While waiting, she prepared them each a salad and took them outside. They ate salad and rolls on the porch.

"So what did you do today?" he asked.

"Worked on the history of the county," she reported, which was true as far as it went. It just wasn't the entire truth. Was that the same as lying by omission? Shunning the philosophical question, she asked about his day.

"I need help at the office on Saturday mornings," he told her. "Will you consider it?"

She knew Ruth filled in for her when he needed staff in the room during examinations and felt a little guilty for guarding her free time so zealously. After all, she had eight more months for her own project before she would be leaving the area.

"Yes."

"Yes you'll consider or yes you'll do it," he demanded at once, beaming a thousand-watt smile her way.

She rolled her eyes and gave up. "I'll do it."

"Good." He leaned over and kissed her.

"But not if you keep that up," she warned.

"I can't make any promises on that score. I've been thinking about us since Zack stopped by and picked up Nicky this morning." His grin was infectious.

He was in a good humor, apparently satisfied with the way his life was going, both in the office and out. She thought of asking his help in her quest as an inexplicable impatience with the task rushed over her.

It came to her that with the past behind her she could plan a future. She tried not to stare at him while she considered just what she wanted in that future.

"Whatever you're thinking of asking," he said softly, "the answer is yes."

She started, nearly spilling the salad in her lap. Her laugh was a little shaky. "Are you a mind reader?"

"With you, I'd like to be."

The husky tone put the questions out of her mind. Instead she thought of better ways to spend the evening. The thought must have appeared in her eyes. They kissed until they realized the steaks were burning. They ate, then kissed some more.

"Shall I stay?" he asked at some point.

"Yes, please."

He chuckled as he lifted her in his arms. "That's what I like about you," he murmured, nuzzling her neck. "You're always so polite."

The cold air blew in the open window of the bedroom but Shelby didn't notice. It was wonderfully warm in bed, sleeping in his arms the whole night through.

On Sunday afternoon Beau took Shelby and Nicky for a horseback ride on the ranch. He put the boy in front of him on his horse. Shelby, he noted, sat comfortably astride a gelding. She'd been totally at ease among the animals as they toured the stables that morning. That pleased him very much. He decided not to analyze the emotion more than that.

They followed a trail up a long sloping ridge until they came out on a bluff. A huge flat-topped rock dominated the area. After tying the horses in a shady spot, he led the way to the stony outcropping.

"We named this the Devil's Dining Room," Beau told them. "That's his table," he said, indicating the van-size flat rock. He pointed to a smaller boulder. "That's his chair."

"There's only one," Nicky said.

"Well, the devil doesn't get much company."

"'Cause nobody likes him." Nicky clamped a hand over his mouth as he giggled.

"Right." Beau lifted his son atop the table, then

steadied Shelby as she stood on the smaller boulder and climbed onto the larger one. He followed her up.

"The view is wonderful," she said, swinging in a circle to look at everything.

In snug-fitting jeans and a royal-blue shirt that matched her eyes, the flame-colored hair partially hidden under a white cowboy hat he'd loaned her, she was about the loveliest woman he'd ever met.

"Yeah, it is," he agreed, without taking his gaze off her.

When she sent a slight frown his way, he grinned and fished out the treat he'd brought in a fanny pack. "Uncle Nick's special everything-but-the-kitchen-sink cookies."

"Mmm, chocolate chips, oatmeal, raisins, walnuts. Delicious," she declared. She sat on the huge boulder and dangled her feet over the edge. "Look, a hawk," she said to Nicky when he sat beside her and did the same.

As usual, after their night of intimacy, she'd withdrawn behind a studied cheeriness. As if she pretended the passion between them had never happened or that it didn't matter.

Did it?

He'd avoided entanglements while he paid off student loans and saved his money to open the clinic. Other than the six weeks he and Nicky's mother had been involved, he hadn't had the time to devote to maintaining a relationship.

Shelby was an intriguing mystery that piqued his

interest and aroused the greatest desire he'd ever felt. Was that love?

Uncle Nick had once said he would know when it came along. He wasn't so sure. He'd thought he was in love with Julie, but that had been nothing like the anticipation, hunger, frustration and pure enjoyment he experienced in his dealings with Shelby.

How she felt about him, he hadn't a clue. Except that she couldn't resist him any more than he could resist her.

Settling on the other side of Nicky, feeling the boy lean trustingly against his side, a funny sensation seized him. Nicky had called him "Dad" last night, emulating the older kids from the R.V. resort, who came over to observe the building of the lodge and to play ball with Nicky.

The idea of home and hearth and family appealed to him, even without Uncle Nick's urging. He studied Shelby as she and Nicky counted the chocolate chips in their cookies to see who had the most.

Was she the one to make his life complete, or was that a romantic fantasy? With the marriages of Zack and Honey, then Travis and Alison, romance was certainly in the air around the Dalton homestead.

"Ready to head back?" he asked when they had finished the snack. The afternoon shadows were long. Evening was coming earlier now that fall was upon them, and the air grew cold with the setting of the sun.

Travis was waiting for them at the stable upon their

return. "Alison says everyone is to come up for dinner. Can you guys make it?"

Beau nodded. "Sure. What time?"

"Whenever you're ready to come over. The food is about ready. Uncle has gone over to help."

Shelby smiled as the two cousins chuckled. Apparently Uncle Nick thought no one could handle food preparation without his direct supervision. She recalled the duel between him and Alison's rather bossy mom over who would be in charge at the wedding reception.

"How did a tough rancher get to be such a mother hen?" she asked when the three of them went into the ranch house to wash up.

"I think it was having six orphans to raise." Beau directed the way to a bathroom in the west wing and supervised Nicky in washing up. "He also became more protective after Tink was kidnapped."

Nicky looked at his father with an anxious expression.

Beau clapped the boy on the shoulder. "That was a long, long time ago, way before you were born. I won't let anyone take you. Did your mom teach you to scream and kick and bite if anyone tries to grab you or force you into a car or truck or anything?"

Nicky shook his head.

"Well," Beau stated, handing the child a towel to dry on, "that's what you do. Kick hard. Bite to hurt. Then the moment you get free, run as fast as you can into a store or to someone's house where you see other people.''

"Even if you don't know them?" Nicky asked.

"Even if you don't know them," Beau said. "Tell them you need help and to call the police. We'll practice so you'll remember what to do."

In a few minutes, walking through the trees to the other house, he leaned close while Nicky ran ahead. "You're quiet. Didn't you approve of my safety lecture?"

"Oh, yes. I had a friend whose father was a karate instructor. He taught her to make noise and fight back. When she was ten, someone did try to grab her on the street, but she fought free. It probably saved her life." She paused, then said, "I think you and your family are going to be good for Nicky. He's already gained in confidence during the short time he's been with you. Children need to know their place in the world."

"Everyone does. Is that what you're looking for?"

She started at the question and stared at him. However she could read nothing in his expression. "What do you mean?"

"You said you wanted to get away, that you were looking for something different. I wondered if Lost Valley fit that description."

"It's lovely here, and certainly a change from the lowlands of the coast." She didn't have to try to think of something more to add since they'd arrived at the other Dalton house at that moment. "Mmm, something smells great."

"Travis smoked a turkey today. It's one of my favorite foods," Beau said, leading the way to a natural stone patio at the side that opened off the kitchen.

"Hello," Alison called to them through the open door. "I thought we'd eat on the patio. This may be the last time before it gets too cold to be outside in the evening."

Shelby saw that a fire had been built in a fire pit at the side of the patio. A curved rock wall behind it reflected the heat back to them. "This is really nice."

"Travis built it," Alison said with obvious pride in her new husband as she came outside with plates in hand. "Would you mind helping Nicky set the table?" She handed the boy the plates as if they did this every day. "I'll get the silver for you."

Shelby placed forks, knives and spoons beside each plate, then she and Nicky folded napkins for each person. Beau, Travis and Uncle Nick each had a beer and discussed the turkey in the smoker.

Beau thought it needed more basting with some kind of sauce. Uncle Nick said you weren't supposed to put anything on smoked meat but the smoke. Travis admitted Alison had had him rub spices into it before putting it on. The uncle allowed that Alison knew what she was doing when it came to cooking.

The smiling bride winked at Shelby when she brought out a huge bowl of corn on the cob and sent

Nicky inside for the butter dish. With chips and salsa, fresh tomatoes and salad, the meal was complete.

At nine, Shelby noticed Nicky covering a huge yawn. It caused her to yawn, too.

"A yawn is the most contagious thing in the world," Beau told them.

She smiled as Alison, then Travis also yawned. She realized she'd smiled all evening as they ate, then sat at the table and talked about the weather, farm prices and the changes taking place in town. Later they'd roasted marshmallows over the fire.

"The town is growing," Beau said.

"Seth should probably open an office here so folks won't have to go to the county seat for everything," Uncle Nick commented.

"We may as well tell him to pack up and move pronto," Travis told her. "When Uncle Nick speaks…"

"Everyone jumps to do his bidding," Beau finished for his cousin.

"That's because Uncle Nick knows everything," Nicky confided, leaning against Shelby as he grew sleepy. "He makes the best cakes and cookies of anybody."

The older man bowed his head graciously and chuckled good-naturedly as the others laughed.

"Okay, young man," Beau said, rising, "it's time to head for home. Tomorrow's a workday."

On the way to town, the sleeping boy nestled against her in the front of the pickup, Shelby mused on the day. It had been great for the child. And for her.

"Thank you for a lovely day," she said softly.

"It was fun, wasn't it?" He flicked her a glance, then turned back to the road. "We could have more of them."

Her heart gave a hitch. "What do you mean?"

"Exactly what you thought. We're good together... at the office, the ranch...and in bed. I think we should be thinking seriously of a future."

"How seriously?" she asked, startled.

"Marriage."

"M-marriage? I hadn't thought—" But she had thought of it, she recalled. She'd decided a serious involvement wasn't possible until she knew more of her past.

"Think about it," he suggested, stopping in front of the cottage by the lake. "I think we'd make a fine family—me, you, Nicky and perhaps a couple more to keep him company."

She was stunned into silence, then, "No, I don't...I don't think that's a good idea."

His gaze was solemn as he studied her in the dim light. "Why not?"

The child sleeping in her arms seemed a heavy weight all at once. She carefully moved aside, laid him down and opened the door. "It isn't possible," she whispered. "Not now."

"When?" Beau immediately demanded.

"I don't know." She fled into the dark house, her

entire body trembling. She knew she was overreacting, but that didn't stop the pain or the doubts that filled her.

Beau had suggested marriage because he was feeling mellow from the lovely evening and their lovemaking the previous night and the happiness of the newlyweds, thus he was thinking of something like that for them, but she wasn't the one who fit into his fanciful scenario.

She couldn't offer him the children he envisioned to complete that perfect family. Not yet. Not until she knew something of her genetic past. Maybe not ever.

Chapter Twelve

Shelby had to give Beau credit for composure. He was the same as usual at the office the next morning.

"Good morning," he said quite cheerfully when she entered at one minute before the hour, waiting in the car until she saw Bertie and Ruth go inside. "You can come on in when you arrive. I promise not to pounce on you."

Bertie snickered from her office.

"Thanks," Shelby managed to say equally casually.

"But don't get overconfident," he added as a warning.

"Is he giving you trouble?" Ruth came out of the lab, her obstetrics case in hand.

"Not a bit," he answered first. "Got a birth?"

"Yes. She and the husband want to have it at home. They think they're pioneers." She rolled her eyes. "Lots of young couples are doing that. It's usually okay, but in this case, I've advised them to at least come in to the clinic. They prefer their place."

"What's worrying you?" he asked.

"High blood pressure." Ruth frowned heavily. "She's on medication, so it's under control."

Shelby knew that during the strain of childbirth, a woman's blood pressure could shoot up to dangerously high levels. Strokes during birth were not unknown.

"If you need me, call," he said.

"We'll bring her in. I've warned them we might have to do that. She's young and otherwise healthy. They want to do this their way. Maybe I'm worrying for nothing."

Shelby checked the four examining rooms for supplies while Beau and the midwife discussed the case. After Ruth left, she called the first patient and the day got underway.

It was almost twelve before she was free to go. Nicky's sitter was going to drop him at school, so she didn't have to wait for him. She ate peanut butter and crackers at her desk at school, then saw those students she'd scheduled for follow-up. At three, she and Nicky returned to the clinic.

Bertie came out on the porch and waved her inside. Turning off the engine, she went into the clinic while the boy joined Bertie's cousin on the porch of the cottage.

"What's wrong?" she asked the receptionist, going into the waiting room.

A young man paced the floor, a look of desperation on his pale face. He didn't seem injured.

"Shelby," Beau called, "we need you in here. Can you help?"

"Of course." She stored her purse and hurried to the lab. Beau was washing up at the sink.

She took one glance and asked, "Surgery?"

"C-section. I'm going to have you handle the anesthesia until the doctor from Council arrives, then I'll need an O.R. nurse. Ruth is assisting."

"Is it her patient from this morning?"

"Yes."

"Stroke?"

"Possibly. She's unconscious. Her blood pressure spiked on the way here. Ruth insisted they come in, but it may be too late." He paused. "The child won't make it."

At his quick glance, she assumed a calm expression. She'd been through this. She knew the risks.

Shelby proceeded to wash up. When they were ready, they went into the operating theater. Ruth was there and assisted with their surgical garb.

The young man in the waiting room must be the woman's husband, Shelby realized. She spared a moment of pity for him. She knew how terrible waiting could be.

Beau instructed her on the procedure to use. The rotation through surgery during her training came back under his expert guidance. When the other doctor arrived, she moved to the end of the table while he took over.

Time ceased to have meaning as the four of them worked together, an almost silent team, fighting for the lives in their care. At last everything was finished.

"I'll stay with her," Shelby volunteered when they moved the woman to the recovery area. She didn't look at the tiny, still bundle of the baby boy that Ruth placed in the nursery cart.

Beau paused beside her. "Are you okay?"

"Yes."

He peered into her eyes as if he could see the truth inside her, touched her shoulder, then continued with his duties. He and the anesthesiologist filled out the necessary papers and signed them. The other doctor glanced toward the waiting room, gave them a sympathetic nod and left.

Beau asked the young husband to come to his office. He shut the door once they were inside.

Shelby recorded the vitals on the sleeping patient. When the woman woke, someone—either Beau or the husband—would have to tell her that all her labor had been in vain. For purely selfish reasons, she was glad it wouldn't be her.

Distancing herself from the useless emotions, she helped Beau finish with the patients who had waited out the interruption. It was seven before the clinic was empty.

"We'll order something from the Crow's Nest," Beau told her, closing the last folder on his desk after completing his notes. "Would you mind doing it? Get something for them, too." He motioned toward the door where they could hear the murmur of voices as the husband and wife talked. Earlier there had been the harsh weeping of deep grief.

Exhaustion made her hands tremble as she dialed the restaurant.

After making sure everyone was fed, she left the clinic and went to the cottage. There she sat on the porch and stared out at the night.

Moonlight cast enchanted coils of silver over the calm lake, but she didn't see the beauty. Exhaustion permeated her mind and body. Despair filled her heart.

During her sojourn in the pediatrics department of a major hospital, the fatality rate among babies had dropped to almost zero. She'd watched for the slightest sign of trouble, had acted promptly and refused to give up if there was any chance at all, but there were times when one had to accept that death was part of the living cycle. Today was one of those.

When the phone rang, she ignored it.

A few minutes later lights glared in her drive, then were gone. It barely registered on her consciousness.

"I thought I'd find you awake," a masculine voice said.

"Beau?" she said, wondering at his presence.

"Yeah." He entered the screened porch and sat beside her on the glider. "It's after midnight."

"What are you doing here? You've had a long day."

"I couldn't sleep."

"Who's with Nicky?"

"I put a monitor beside his bed. Ruth will go to him if he wakes."

She forced her own grief at bay. "How's the patient?"

"Fine. She may have had a ministroke, but there are no signs of damage. She'll see a specialist in Boise tomorrow. It's you I'm worried about."

"Me?"

"I think you take it personally when...when things don't go right. It was out of our hands from the first."

She started to protest, then fell silent. "It's so unfair," she whispered.

"I know." He stroked down her hair.

"To work so hard, to go through so much and for what? Nothing. It doesn't matter how much you dream and wish and hope—"

She stopped and sucked in a ragged breath. He slipped an arm around her and pulled her close.

"I can handle this," she insisted, fighting the tears that threatened to choke her. "I can. I have before."

"Things were different today."

She folded her arms across her middle and held herself together by willpower. "How?"

"We'd talked about marriage and children last night. That, coupled with today, threw you into the past and your own tragedy." He tipped her chin up and gazed into her eyes in the dim light. "Not many births end that way. You love babies. You should have some of your own."

She shook her head violently. "Never," she said. "Never again. I couldn't."

He became very still, as if every part of him had frozen, then he stroked her hair very gently as if to comfort her. "What happened to your baby?" he asked quietly. "Perhaps it's time you talked about it."

Her first impulse was to deny any idea of what he was talking about, but meeting his eyes, she realized she'd given too much away. "How did you know?"

"Stretch marks on your breasts, one across your back."

She carefully placed the glass on the old wicker table as if her life depended upon getting it exactly in that spot. Her thoughts were in a swirl, yet her mind felt painfully blank.

"She died," she finally said. "Ten years ago."

He exhaled audibly. "What happened?"

She stared at the play of moonlight on the nearly smooth surface of the lake. It took a conscious effort to open her mouth and force out the words. "She had a metabolic disorder. She faded gradually until she went in a coma one night and never woke up."

His hand clasped hers. "I'm sorry."

She pulled away and crossed her arms, holding in all the pain from that long-ago time. "I thought I would die, too, but...I discovered life has a way of holding on."

"But it hurts," he said softly, pity in his glance. "Where was the father during all this?"

"He left. When she was a month old." She spoke in disjointed phrases, hardly able to sustain a complete thought. "She cried a lot at first. Then she didn't. She grew too weak. And then she died."

Silence filled the porch, rising like slow floodwaters until it covered her ears and she couldn't hear the chirp of crickets or the faint croon of the wind anymore. She waited, knowing the pain would ease if she only held on.

"Ten years," he murmured. "You were nineteen, a big burden for one so young."

"My parents were there. And his mom. She was our neighbor. We married, Brent and I, as soon as I got out of school. He'd graduated the year before. He'd been my friend all my life, but he couldn't take the crying."

Beau spoke softly, "Yeah. The helplessness is the worst thing. Watching a person weaken and fade and knowing there's not a thing you can do to stop it."

She looked at him then. "Yes, that was the worst thing. And not understanding why, why this child had to suffer, why she was taken when I loved her so."

No more words would come. The world blurred as the long-suppressed tears fought their way to the surface. She'd done her weeping, for all the good it did, ten years ago. What was the point now?

Hands, strong, gentle, insistent, stroked her.

"Don't," she whispered. "Please. Don't."

He held her hand between both of his. "We've shared the most intimate of physical contact. Don't shut me out now."

His voice was deep and soothing. He stroked her hair and down her back until the murky waters of past despair and the need to weep dissipated. For a long time they simply sat there and watched the moonlight on the lake.

"It's okay," he said. "Tears, anger—it's natural to feel those."

She couldn't hide the dredges of bitterness. "It doesn't change anything."

"No," he agreed on a sad note, "it doesn't change anything, but recognizing our feelings can help us move on."

She rubbed her eyes. "I've done that."

"That's why you became a pediatrics nurse," he said, a thoughtful frown etching a deeper line between his eyes.

"Yes. I thought I could help other babies, other parents, when things were difficult for them."

He nodded. "You and your husband divorced after he left?"

"Not right then, but after the baby died."

She didn't add that everything had ended on that

day—her marriage, her expectations, her time for being young.

"I'll never go through that again," she vowed in a low, ragged voice, wanting him to know she meant it.

"Then," he said evenly, "you're a coward."

When he let her go and stood, she became aware of the chill night air that flowed all around her.

She flung up her head and met his angry gaze. "Yes," she said, and he would never know how hard it was for her to utter that one word.

Long after he left, she sat there, shivering from the wretched, lonely cold.

For the rest of the week she did her work, took Nicky to school when she went and brought him to the clinic at the end of the school day. The sitter stayed with him at the cottage until the doctor was free.

Shelby regained her poise as she realized he had again backed off, maybe permanently this time, and was giving her space to work out the questions and problems in her own mind. The Dalton men were truly remarkable. No wonder women fell hard for them.

On Wednesday morning she lay in bed and listened to rain on the roof. A storm had blown in during the night, heralded by a cold wind out of the northwest. Twice during the night, she'd heard hail striking the window of the bedroom. She'd had to put an extra blanket on the bed.

If Beau had been there, she could have curled up against him and been warm enough.

Her sigh was loud in the silent room. He despised her for what he perceived as her cowardly refusal to go on with her life. Her parents worried about her for the same reason. None of them understood her fears.

She'd watched one child die because of her. She wouldn't take a chance on another inheriting the same fate.

So, yes, she was a coward.

For the first time since she'd arrived over two months ago, the air was so strained between her and Beau that even Bertie and Ruth noticed. The two woman kept giving her little worried glances, then shaking their heads as if wondering about her mental balance.

On Saturday she regretted agreeing to come in, but she rose, dressed and reported to the office at eight. A person kept her word, her parents had taught her. At noon, when the last patient was gone, she checked supplies, made sure the medicine cabinet was locked and prepared to leave.

Outside she met Nicky. "Hi, cowboy, how's it going?" she said, noting the new boots, jeans and hat he wore.

"Great. We're going to the ranch. Uncle Nick said to invite you, too. We're going to grill hamburgers."

"That sounds lovely. Tell your uncle I said thanks, but I have a meeting later today."

"You can't come?"

He looked so woebegone she almost changed her mind, but thinking of Beau's withdrawn countenance, she shook her head. "Not this time. Maybe next."

She left him sitting on the top porch step, waiting for his father, his eyes solemn as he watched her leave. She wondered if she would make it through the long winter until her contract ended next June.

Beau spotted his son on the porch when he went out. "Where's your sitter?" he asked, not spotting the woman.

"She had to leave for a 'pointment. Bertie said I could sit out here where she could see me instead of inside."

"I see. Ready to head out?"

"Yes, sir."

Beau noted the boy looked disconsolate. "Anything you need to talk about?" he asked on the way to the resort. They were going to eat, then work for a couple of hours before driving out to the ranch for dinner.

Nicky, his young face wearing a frown, thought it over before he spoke. "If you like somebody, how do you let them know—I mean, if you don't want to say it?"

Beau started to smile, but glancing at the earnest expression on Nicky's face, he realized this was very serious to the boy. Thinking of his own not too successful love life, he was sympathetic.

"How do you make someone like you back?" Nicky added. "I mean, special…better'n anybody else?"

The kid had it bad. Like his old man.

Beau tried to think of helpful advice. "Well, I think first you have to listen, really listen, when she talks to you. Also, you should talk about what she's interested in some of the time."

"What about presents?"

"Girls like flowers and candy." He thought of a five-year-old's finances. "Even a pretty rock can be nice."

"One that's all sparkly?"

Diamonds came to mind. "Yeah," Beau said. "You have someone special you want to impress?"

Nicky hesitated, then said, "Shelby's birthday is next month. I heard her and my teacher talking about it. Do you think she's old?"

"Ah, no, not too old. Thirty isn't ancient."

Nicky visibly relaxed. When Beau parked beside the resort, both he and his son looked next door to see if the woman in question was visible. She wasn't.

Beau smiled at the irony. He and his son were in love with the same person. He'd thought Shelby felt the same about them, but…well, whatever her feelings, they weren't strong enough to overcome the past.

He and Nicky went to the restaurant for lunch, then

returned to the lodge to work on the caulking. Things were moving along rapidly on this project. The outside walls were up and wrapped, the roof was almost done.

With siding, windows and doors installed, they would be ready for winter weather and the inside finish work. That would take them into spring. They planned on Memorial Day for the grand opening celebration. Roni was already planning an advertising campaign and setting up the website.

Now all they had to do was settle on a name. Lost Valley Lodge was his choice. Roni and Uncle Nick went for Seven Devils Inn. The rest had no preference. Maybe he'd ask Shelby. As soon as they were speaking again.

At four, he told Nicky they should call it a day and head out to the ranch. Before they reached the pickup, Shelby came around a stand of pines, her ponytail swinging to and fro as she jogged toward the cottage.

Their eyes met and held for a long ten seconds before she looked at Nicky. Her mouth bloomed into a smile. Beau thought he just might be jealous of a five-year-old.

"Hi," he said when she stopped near them.

"Hi. You two must have been working on the lodge. It's going up fast." She blotted her face on the end of her T-shirt, exposing an enticing inch of skin at her waist.

"It's still several months from completion, but my helper and I are doing our part."

Nicky looked pleased when Beau included him. The boy had powers of concentration that still amazed him in one so young. For his age, Nicky was patient and meticulous. He seemed to prefer working alongside the men to playing with the kids at the R.V. resort.

Beau thought of his own life, surrounded by relatives who'd cared for him. He was sure Nicky had been with adults most of his life and had learned to entertain himself.

"Uncle Nick's going to be mad if you don't come out with us," he now said to Shelby. "You'll get a lecture if you show up for church tomorrow."

"Yeah," Nicky agreed. "You'd better come."

She glanced from one to the other. Beau waited out the internal battle he could see in her eyes. When she sighed, he knew the appeal of the boy had won out over her better sense. But when she looked at him, he realized the answer was negative.

"I can't," she said to Nicky. "Not today."

"Okay," the boy said, giving her his stoic smile.

Leaving in the pickup a minute later, Beau said, "It takes real courage to smile in the face of disappointment. I was proud of you back there."

When he glanced over at Nicky, his heart lurched once before resuming a normal beat. The boy was grinning, an honest, ear-to-ear, beaming grin that sent a shaft of paternal love straight to a father's soul.

"She wanted to come," Nicky said confidently. "She just had something else she had to do."

Sunday morning the sun was barely up when Shelby picked up her purse and keys. Going to her car, she jumped when a cricket leaped up in front of her. She wasn't doing anything wrong, so why did she feel so nervy?

Parking in plain view in the clinic parking lot, she defended her decision as hurting no one. She used her key to enter the side door, locked it behind her and went upstairs to the attic rooms.

The air was chill, but the first light was streaming in the windows and would soon warm up the space. She now knew the name she was looking for. The retired minister was James Thorneson. His wife was Sandra. James had retired at sixty-four and been thirteen years older than his wife. Sandra's mother had been a Pickford before her marriage.

Could Sandra Thorneson have been the young widow Sandra Silvers?

Riffling systematically through the files, she searched for information. Finally she found the folder she was interested in. Heart thundering, she opened the file for Sandra Thorneson and began to read.

The record went back to the girl's birth, first under a doctor Shelby had never heard of, then as a young married woman under the care of Dr. Barony who had been new to the practice at that time.

At last she leaned against the wall and stared at the peaks now flooded with sunlight. Sandra Thorneson, over a period of fifteen years had suffered three miscarriages. As Miss Pickford had said, she and her husband had had no children. Sandra had also suffered from varying degrees of depression that had apparently started with her first miscarriage. The doctor had recommended therapy, but the patient had steadfastly refused.

Had the minister's wife been unable to carry other children because of the guilt at giving up her love child?

There was only one person who possibly had the answers to her questions. If Shelby explained her quest, would the retired teacher tell her what she wanted to know?

"Finding anything?" a masculine baritone asked.

Every nerve in Shelby's body jerked guiltily. "Beau," she said weakly. She clutched the file in her hand, but it was too late to try to hide it.

He took it from her, looked at the name and read through the file. "Why?" he asked, returning it.

Shelby suddenly agreed with Miss Pickford. Sometimes it was better to let the past stay buried.

"Are you looking for your birth mother?"

She couldn't stop the startled glance. With a defeated sigh, she knew the time had come to share her past. "How did you know I had a birth mother?"

"You tried to track the owner of a piece of jewelry, plus you let Trek Lanigan think your mother was dead, but I knew she wasn't. Those facts, coupled with your rather intense interest in the residents of the area and your rather flimsy reasons for moving here, were enough to spur my curiosity."

"I see."

Beau sat beside her on the floor. He placed a mug of coffee near her feet, then sipped from his.

"Where's Nicky?"

"I asked Uncle Nick to take him to the ranch from Sunday School, then I came back here. I saw your car in the parking lot and was pretty sure I knew why."

"I don't want to cause pain to anyone. I just wanted to know...a few things."

"Such as?"

"If there were any genetic disorders in the family."

He digested that. "Because of your baby?"

"Yes."

"What about the father's family?"

She moved her head against the wall negatively. "We knew his family. Besides, he has another child, a little girl. She's normal."

"So you concluded the problem had to be you," he said grimly. "Things happen. No one knows why. It doesn't have to be anyone's fault."

"But it could be."

"Yeah, it could be." He rubbed the rim of the mug with his thumb. "You won't rest until you know as much as possible, so how can I help?"

She'd thought of asking for his help more than once. Reaching into her purse, she retrieved the notebook and flipped it open. "Do you know where this mine is?"

He looked at the location she'd copied from the

claim. "Zack or Travis probably do. You got hiking shoes?"

"Yes."

"Let me change, then we'll go."

After both of them had changed to appropriate hiking clothes, she rode with him to the ranch. There they consulted the other two men. Uncle Nick demanded to know what was going on. He also insisted they all have lunch before the food grew cold.

"Shelby is adopted. She wants to find out about her birth parents, if possible," Beau explained when they were seated at the dining table.

The other two women were fascinated. Alison said she might be able to help since her father, being a senator, had lots of contacts. "Do you know anything about them?"

Shelby showed them the bracelet and told them of the widow who'd given her child up for reasons unknown. She hesitated, unsure if she could share the rest.

A warm hand clasped her shoulder. "You don't have to say anything else," Beau told her.

"They may as well know it all."

At his nod, she began, choosing her words carefully since Nicky was present. She revealed all she knew and why she wanted to know more. When she told about the baby, she clenched her hands in her lap and willed her voice to be steady. Beau laid his hand over hers. It became easier to talk. There was silence when she finished.

"Let's see the claim," Travis said. "Yeah," he said, looking it over, "I know where this is—over near your sister's place," he said to his wife.

"We can get there by horseback in an hour," Zack told Shelby. "I have some great mountain mounts."

They all looked at her.

She inhaled carefully, not sure, at this point, that she wanted to know more. She found she was afraid that, should she discover the truth, she might wish she hadn't.

Like Pandora's box, once opened she wouldn't be able to stuff all the ills back inside and slam the lid.

"Yes," she finally said. "I want to go."

"Great," Nicky piped up. "Did you know I have a horse of my own now?"

She gazed at him, eager to ride off on a great adventure. "That's wonderful," she said, taking his hand. "Let's go."

Uncle Nick decided he wouldn't be left behind. In a few minutes, Shelby found herself riding off into the Seven Devils Mountains, escorted by seven Daltons.

Chapter Thirteen

"There's a cabin," Shelby said, spotting it among a stand of trees.

"It was an old mining shack," Travis told her. "The forest rangers use it now to store supplies and also for a snow cabin in case someone gets stranded up here."

"Where's the mine?"

"We'll have to hike from here," he said.

With Travis leading the way, the little party hiked up a steep trail for three hundred feet. The mine was hacked out of the side of the mountain in a quartz vein running through granite and basalt. The mine was nothing more than a narrow, shallow cavern.

"There's nothing here," Shelby said in disappointment.

She must have sounded woebegone because Nicky moved closer and took her hand. She couldn't manage a smile, not even for him.

"I thought there would be something." She really didn't know what she expected—maybe a ghost town in which she would discover artifacts left by the miners who'd come through the area over the past hundred and fifty years.

"Let's check the snow cabin," Zack suggested. "Silvers would have stayed there most likely."

Shelby followed the rest down the steep trail. She really had no hope at all of discovering anything more about her past, but she didn't want to dampen the spirits of the group, who looked upon the quest as an adventure.

The door to the cabin wasn't locked. The special catch helped bear-proof it, but it presented no problem to the Dalton men. Travis stepped aside and let her go in. Uncle Nick was right behind.

"Wait," she heard Beau say, but he wasn't talking to her.

While the rest stayed outside, Shelby and Uncle Nick explored the cabin. Furniture was minimal. Bunk beds lined the longer walls. A table was in the middle of the room. Four stumps served as chairs. A potbellied iron stove sat on a thin slab of rock opposite the door. Four shelves were located to the right of the stove.

They also found two barrels. One contained gray wool blankets. The other held cans of supplies—coffee, soup, a tin of crackers and one of matches—that would get a person through a storm. There was wood for the stove.

She turned in a slow circle. "That's all that's here."

"I think I see something on the top shelf," Uncle Nick said, craning his neck to see. "Let's get a stool over here and look."

Shelby rolled the section of log over, then climbed up on it. Uncle Nick steadied her with a hand on her arm. She spotted an object in the corner.

Dust covered the shelf and the metal box, making her sneeze as she stepped down. "It's a box."

"Open it," he urged, obviously impatient to do so.

Shelby pulled the metal hasp free and lifted the lid. A box of stick matches rested on top of some yellowed newspaper articles. She set the box on the table and lifted out the items. The newspaper clippings she recognized.

"I've seen these," she said, her fingers trembling slightly as they looked at the articles detailing Ralph Silvers' gold find. There was a photo of the miner that Shelby had missed in her search. Since it wasn't in color, she couldn't tell anything except that his hair looked dark.

But there was a real photograph under the clippings, one that was in color, although it had begun to turn sepia-toned.

"Oh," Shelby said softly.

Uncle Nick peered over her shoulder. "That's one

of the Pickford girls,'' he said. "No, that's the younger girl's daughter,'' he corrected upon studying it more closely. "She married the preacher from the Methodist church.''

Shelby wasn't sure if the older man disapproved of the preacher or the marriage. "Did you know them?''

"Yes. He was a lot older than she was.''

"It wasn't a good marriage?''

He shrugged, then grinned. "Well, he wasn't to my taste, but they got along well enough.''

Shelby studied the face of the young woman in the photo. Her hair was dark auburn and her eyes were blue. As blue as her own, Shelby realized.

She tucked it into her shirt pocket and put the box back on the shelf. "We'd better go.''

Outside, the family was admiring the view from the steep mountainside and picking out landmarks. They turned as one when they heard the door close.

"Did you find anything?'' Nicky asked.

She hesitated then nodded. "A picture.'' She handed it around. The Dalton clan peered at the woman, then at her.

Beau handed it back. "Let's get home. There's a cloud forming over He-Devil peak.''

No one asked her any questions on the trip to the ranch, for which she was grateful. After saying their farewells, she, Beau and Nicky returned to town.

"Do you want to have dinner with us?'' he asked when they arrived at her cottage.

"No, thank you. I want to…think,'' she finished.

He frowned at her refusal, but didn't argue. "Right. See you in the morning."

She nodded and went into the cabin. She waited only until the pickup was well out of sight, then she changed her hiking boots for jogging shoes and started down the path toward town. Arriving at the neat old house belonging to Miss Pickford fifteen minutes later, she paused on the sidewalk, her heart loud in her ears.

The hose was running on the flower bed next to the front steps. A watering can sat on the porch. No one answered her rap on the old-fashioned door knocker shaped like a lion's head.

An eerie sensation crept along her spine. She walked around to the back of the house. A lone figure bent over the tomato vines in the garden. Miss Pickford straightened when she saw Shelby approach.

"Miss Pickford," she said and paused, unsure of what to say next.

The older woman's breast rose and fell in a deep sigh. "We'll go inside," she said.

Shelby followed her into the kitchen of the elegant old house. Miss Pickford placed the basket of cherry tomatoes on a side table and washed her hands. After removing her apron, she poured two glasses of iced tea, gave one to Shelby, then led the way into what could only be called the parlor.

"What do you want to know?" she asked when they were seated on identical chairs. The chairs, sofa and marble-topped tables in the room all matched in the harp-shaped curves and carvings on the wood.

Shelby removed the picture from her pocket. "Is this your cousin's daughter?"

The other woman glanced at the photo without touching it and nodded.

"Was she my mother, my birth mother?" Shelby asked.

"Yes."

Anger flamed, quick and hot, in Shelby. "You saw the bracelet. You knew what I wanted to know when I was here before. Why didn't you tell me then?"

"It wasn't my secret to share," Miss Pickford explained, her tone gentle but unapologetic. "I'd given my word to Sandra to keep her confidence."

"She's dead. What does it matter?"

"Her mother, my first cousin, is still alive. Sandra never wanted her to know she'd made such a foolish mistake."

Shelby had accepted long ago that her birth had been a mistake, but to hear it spoken out loud hurt in ways she hadn't expected. "I'd like to know about it," she now said as coolly as she could.

"Why?"

"Because I had a child who had a metabolism disorder. There's a possible genetic influence involved. Before I risk having more children, I want to know I'm not passing on a gene that contributes to their deaths."

Her words finally got through to Miss Pickford.

"I'm so sorry," she murmured. She gestured help-lessly. "The story is old and trite due to its common occurrence."

"I still want to hear it."

"Sandra was going with the minister and we were all expecting an announcement of their engagement at any time. Then Ralph Silvers came to town. He was a handsome, worldly daredevil. Just the thing to turn a young girl's head, especially since she'd never been more than a hundred miles from home."

Shelby knew the rest of the story. The seduction. The gold mine that didn't pan out. The charmer who quietly left town after his dreams failed, leaving a brokenhearted lover behind.

"When Sandra confessed to me, she was already six months pregnant. Dr. Barony contacted a medical school roommate. I arranged for Sandra to accompany me on a trip that summer. I think you know the rest."

The tale wasn't as tragic nor as sordid as Shelby had feared it might be. "So she returned here and married the minister?"

"Yes, the next summer they were wed…in the rose garden here at this house, in fact. I don't think he ever understood why she preferred the garden over the church."

"Guilt," Shelby supplied. Fatigue rolled over her. "Did Silvers give her the bracelet?"

"Yes. It was special for her, with love knots and the mountain columbines entwined."

"I see."

"I hope you don't hate her," Miss Pickford said quietly. "She'd been such a dreamy young girl, but then she had to grow up in a hurry. She changed after that, becoming the ideal minister's wife, but for a long, long time, each year on your birthday, she cried. I know that for a fact."

"I don't hate her," Shelby said. "I had a wonderful life. My parents are the best, loving and kind...and worried about me. I have to call them."

"Are you going to tell them about your findings?"

"Yes. So they'll know I'm okay. I owe them that much. I don't suppose you know anything of Ralph Silvers?"

"Only what he told us. He never mentioned any problems with children in the family. There weren't any in your mother's family."

She nodded. She placed the untasted glass of tea on the marble-topped table. "Thank you." She hesitated. "You needn't worry. I won't be telling any secrets. I wanted to know for my own peace of mind."

Without waiting for an answer, she walked out the door and down the street until she reached the lake path. There she turned toward the snug house that waited for her.

Home. It had a wonderful ring to it.

And no wonder. She'd been on a thirty-year trip to get here. It came to her that she hadn't made it yet.

Taking in a deep breath, she turned once more and headed down another path, one that took her to a quaint old Victorian like most of the houses in the town. Behind it was another cottage, smaller than the one where she lived, but bigger in its heart.

Because its heart was that of a man who had compassion and love enough to share with a woman who'd been afraid to share hers and plenty left over for a child who needed somewhere to belong.

He stepped onto the porch before she was halfway across the lawn. Holding the screen door open, he waited.

"Hi," she said huskily.

He gazed into her eyes for a long second. "Welcome," he said. "We grilled hamburgers. There's one extra. You want it?"

"Yes, please."

Nicky was at the dining table. His smile lit up his face. "Hi, Shelby," he said. "These hamburgers are really good. Dad and I cooked them."

Beau brought in a chair from the porch. He and Nicky made room for her at the table. They chatted about the day as they ate.

"Did you find out everything you wanted to know?" Beau asked, his beautiful eyes looking at her with warmth...yes, definitely with warmth.

She shivered delicately.

He smiled.

"I did," she told them. "Did I tell you about being adopted?" she asked Nicky. "I have the most wonderful parents in the world. They love me very much, the way your daddy loves you."

Nicky nodded in complete understanding.

"The way Nicky and his dad love a certain red-headed temptress," Beau said softly.

"Here they come," Nicky whispered excitedly.

"I see 'em," Beau replied.

"What are you two conspiring about?" Shelby demanded, standing back to admire their handiwork.

For three hours they'd been busy arranging the new furniture in the four upstairs rooms. Three were now outfitted as bedrooms with pretty sheets, comforters and curtains to match while the fourth and largest was a family room complete with television, sofa and chairs, bookcases and an old-fashioned secretary of cherry with the most interesting nooks and crannies in it.

After a week of rain, the first Saturday in October had dawned sunny and warm. Along a tiny seasonal creek at the back of the yard the cottonwoods had changed to brilliant gold. Farther up the mountains, aspen trees shimmered as if their branches were filled with butterflies.

"We aren't conspiring," the boy said, then giggled like mad.

"There's someone here," Beau told her.

She peered past him at the parking lot of the clinic. A car had stopped there. The clinic had closed for the day, and she hoped there was no emergency to spoil the afternoon.

Another vehicle pulled in behind the first. Then another. Shelby stared as the occupants got out. What she saw made no sense.

"Mom? Dad?" she said.

She blinked, but the older couple, accompanied by the entire Dalton gang, were still there, coming up the sidewalk. She rushed down the stairs and outside, Beau and Nicky hot on her heels.

Her parents came onto the porch, taking her into their arms and giving her hugs and kisses the likes of which she'd never had before. Stunned, she hugged them back.

"Happy birthday," Nicky shouted in her ear as he took his turn giving her a bone-crushing embrace.

"Oh. Oh, it is my birthday, isn't it?" She turned to the two most important men in her life. "Did you guys plan this?" At Beau's and Nicky's nods, she continued, "They never said a word to me, not a clue. I had no idea any of you were coming."

"That's okay," Roni assured her. "Uncle Nick has been baking for three days. We have your birthday dinner."

Shelby couldn't stop smiling. "Beau told me not to worry about anything to eat. I thought that meant he was going to order in pizza."

"Huh," Uncle Nick said. "We're having *real* food."

In the kitchen behind the clinic, they warmed barbecued pork and baked beans. With homemade rolls, slaw and potato salad, it was the best meal Shelby had ever had.

It was after Shelby made a wish and blew out the candles that someone knocked on the side door. There was an instant's hush among the noisy group, then Beau went to the door. "Come in," they heard him say.

He returned to the kitchen. Miss Pickford was with him. She smiled gravely at Shelby and held out a package. "I think these belong to you," she said.

Shelby opened the wrapping and found a jeweler's box inside. Opening it, she stared at a pair of earrings that matched the bracelet she wore. "Where did you get them?"

"Sandra. Before she and James moved to Arizona, she gave them to me. I'd forgotten about them until now."

"Put them on," Beau said, and fastened them in her ears. "Very pretty."

"Did Shelby belong to your cousin's girl?" Uncle Nick wanted to know.

Miss Pickford nodded and smiled. "Shelby and I are third cousins," she said, bringing the relationship out into the open.

"Actually," Shelby's mom corrected, "that would be first cousin, twice removed."

"What? How's that?" the uncle demanded.

Mrs. Wheeling elaborated. "If Miss Pickford and Shelby's grandmother were first cousins, then Shelby's birth mother would be Miss Pickford's first cousin, once removed, which makes her Shelby's first cousin, twice removed."

"What happened to second and third cousins?" the old man asked.

"The children of first cousins are second cousins to each other," Mrs. Wheeling explained in her soft Kentucky drawl, her tone authoritative.

Uncle Nick was fascinated. "Is that right?"

"I believe it is," Miss Pickford agreed. "Since we're first cousins, you should call me by my given name."

Roni had a question. "If Shelby is related to Miss Pickford and Miss Pickford is related to the Daltons, does that mean Shelby is kin to us?"

"Shelby is related to the Pickford side of the family," Miss Pickford said with a twinkle in her light blue eyes, "not the rowdy Daltons."

That brought protests and much laughter from the crowd. After cake and ice cream, the Daltons decamped for the ranch. Shelby saw her parents upstairs to the guest bedroom while Beau put his son to bed in his new room with its colorful cowboy motif.

He wondered if Shelby would stay with him or if he should go to the cottage behind the big house. They had lived very circumspectly since last Saturday when she'd come to him with her complete story. After all, there was only so much even the most ardent couple could do with a five-year-old nearby.

"Everything all set?" he asked, finding Shelby in the family room after Nicky was tucked in.

"Yes. My folks love the house."

"Come'ere, you," he said, unable to stay away another moment. He kissed her until she was breathless. She kissed him back until he was breathless. "Very nice," he murmured, nuzzling the spot behind her ear. "I have something for you."

"You already gave me a present downstairs."

He'd given her a pair of cowgirl boots and a hat of her own. "That was for everyone to see. This one is private."

He removed the box from the drawer where he'd hidden it earlier and took out the ring. "Nicky was in on this, but he said it was okay if I gave it to you when we were alone."

She nodded, her eyes on his. Her lips, beautiful and sensuous, trembled a little when she smiled. He took her left hand and slipped the ring on.

"How soon can we marry? I'm not sure how much longer I can hold out without throwing you on an examining table and ravishing you on the spot."

Snuggled in his arms, his engagement ring on her finger, Shelby thought she might never move again. Then his words hit home. "How about starting now?" She nibbled on his ear.

His breath caught in his throat. "I was wondering if you would send me to the cottage."

"I can't. I'm too starved."

Arm in arm, they went to the room they would share for the next thirty or forty years, maybe more. Barring accidents, Daltons tended to live a long time. He wanted every minute to be with this woman.

Taking it slow and easy, well, as much as he

could.. *she* wasn't being very cooperative in the slow department—he made love to the woman who had fascinated him from the moment he'd met her. From the very first moment.

He'd never experienced that before. Uncle Nick had known what he was talking about when he said Beau would know when real love came along. He did.

"I love you," he whispered again and again.

She answered back every time. "I love you, too."

An eternity later they rested in each other's arms. "What about children?" he asked. "Nicky asked this morning if we'd get some more soon. He said he wanted two brothers."

"How about two boys and a girl?"

He leaned on an elbow so he could look into her eyes. "You mean that? You're not afraid?"

"I do mean it." Shelby gazed at him with all the love in her heart. "I'm sure I'll worry until I hold a perfectly healthy baby in my arms, but I'm willing to take a chance. If you are."

"With you, I'll take any risk."

She cupped his lean jaw and lightly brushed her thumb over his wonderful lips that delivered such magical kisses.

"You were right when you said I was a coward. After I talked to Peggy Sue—I'll never get used to calling Miss Pickford by that name!—I realized my mother had been afraid to face the scandal and shock her pregnancy would cause in a small town. I think she paid for it the rest of her life."

"Yes," he said. "She never carried another child to term."

"I once read that people regret the things they didn't do more than the ones they did. I realized I didn't want to live my life without you, no matter what it had in store for us."

He touched her breasts that had once nursed a child, and pictured their own little one there. "I once asked Uncle Nick about love," he told her. "He said I would know when the one and only true love came along. He was right. For me, that's you."

She nodded, believing him, this man who was as steadfast as the protective hills surrounding them. "I came here to find my past. I found the future—you."

* * * * *

Which Dalton will end up with Amelia?
Find out in
FOUND IN LOST VALLEY (SE 1560),
coming from Special Edition
this August!

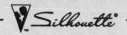

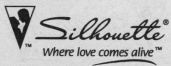

Coming in June 2003

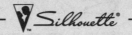

SPECIAL EDITION™

Alaskan Nights
by JUDITH LYONS

Silhouette Special Edition #1547

It all started with a fire in the cockpit. Winnie Mae Taylor
could handle that. But could she put out the fire in her heart
that her mysterious passenger, Rand Michaels, had ignited?
After a crash landing, they had some time to find out if they
could handle the wilderness, the secrets they kept from each
other and being on the run....

**Look for another Silhouette Special Edition novel
from Judith Lyons in 2004!**

*Available at your favorite retail outlet.
Only from Silhouette Books!*

Where love comes alive™

From *USA TODAY* bestselling author

EMILIE RICHARDS

**comes the story of a woman who has played life
by the book, and now the rules have changed.**

Faith Bronson, daughter of a prominent Virginia senator and wife
of a charismatic lobbyist, finds her privileged life shattered when
her marriage ends abruptly. Only just beginning to face the lie
she has lived, she finds sanctuary with her two children in a
run-down row house in exclusive Georgetown. This historic
house harbors deep secrets of its own, secrets that force Faith
to confront the deceit that has long defined her.

PROSPECT STREET

"Richards adds to the territory
staked out by such authors as
Barbara Delinsky and Kristin Hannah....
Richards' writing is unpretentious and
effective and her characters burst with
vitality and authenticity."

—*Publishers Weekly*

*Available the first week of June 2003
wherever paperbacks are sold!*

New York Times Bestselling Author

LISA JACKSON

A TWIST OF FATE

When Kane Webster buys First Puget Bank, he knows he is buying trouble. Someone is embezzling funds, and the evidence points to Erin O'Toole. Kane is determined to see her incriminated—until he meets her. He didn't expect to feel such an intense attraction to Erin—or to fall in love with her.

After her divorce, Erin has no desire to get involved with anyone—especially not her new boss. But she can't resist Kane Webster. Before she can help it, she's swept into a passionate affair with a man she barely knows…a man she already loves. But when she discovers Kane's suspicions, she must decide—can she stay with a man who suspects her of criminal intent?

"A natural talent!" —*Literary Times*

Available the first week of June 2003 wherever paperbacks are sold!

MLJ705

Have you ever wanted to be part of a romance reading group?

Be part of the Readers' Ring, Silhouette Special Edition's exciting book club!

Don't miss the next title!

BALANCING ACT

by Lilian Darcy
(SE #1552)
Available July 2003

Encourage your friends to engage in lively discussions by using the suggested reading group questions provided at the end of the novel. Also, visit the **www.readersring.com** Web site for engaging interactive materials related to this novel.

Available at your favorite retail outlet.

Silhouette®
™ *Where love comes alive*™

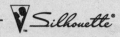